SEDUCING
THE
WARRIR

VIRGINIE
MARCONATO

OLIVERHEBERBOOKS

Seducing the Warrior Copyright 2024 © Virginie Marconato

Cover art by Dar Albert at Wicked Smart Designs

Published by Oliver-Heber Books

0 9 8 7 6 5 4 3 2 1

PROLOGUE

Was she making a mistake?

Eyja's hand tightened over the knife's handle. No, she wasn't. It had to be done, her hair was just too long to pass as a boy's, so it had to go. There was no other choice. In any case, the length of her tresses hardly defined who she was. Her indomitable spirit did, and she would prove it forthwith.

With slow deliberation, she cut the first lock of hair. It would grow back soon enough anyway.

Everyone berated her for her lack of feminine grace and delicacy, calling her boyish but really, after growing up surrounded by three brothers and their friends, what else was she supposed to be? And why was it such a problem to be strong in mind and body anyway? If she'd been a boy, she would have been praised for her grit and resourcefulness. But because she was a female, people expected her to be gentle, soft-spoken and calm. No one saw that it took great determination and stamina on her part to keep up with a band of men in their prime.

Well, she was about to put these two underrated qualities to good use. Dressed as a man amidst other men bent on a mission, she would not stand out for once. She would be judged on her courage and ability alone, not her sex. It would be quite liberating, she imagined.

But first, she had to make herself look like a man.

Another lock of hair fell at her feet.

The clothes she was wearing felt loose, and unfortunately she had no way of knowing how she appeared in them but she was not unduly worried. As far as people were concerned, someone with short hair and braies was a man, and that was all there was to it. They wouldn't look at her twice, as they would be too busy worrying about the battle ahead. Yes, she was confident they would take her on, glad of every recruit they could find. After all, the more people joined the army, the better their chance at victory.

By a stroke of luck this morning she had overheard Moon, one of her brothers' friends, mention his desire to join the army King Harold had assembled to go and stop the Norse invaders who'd landed on their shores earlier this month. Born in this country to a Dane father and a Saxon mother, Moon had explained to Torsten that he wished to stop the raiders who would wreck the land and cause innocent people to suffer.

She understood his reasoning and shared his urge to defend their country. Her own father, Wolf, was an Icelander, who'd found a home here after being sent into exile more than thirty years ago, and married a Saxon as well. Eyja was therefore in the same situation as Moon, and if she could help, then she would.

The last lock of hair fell to the floor in silence. There, the transformation was complete, and the die was cast.

She was going to war.

CHAPTER ONE

EAST ANGLIA, SEPTEMBER 1066

Had he made the right decision?

Moon's jaw tightened. Yes. No matter what people might say, there was no other path for him. He had to go, or he would not be able to live with his conscience.

Around him all the men were tense, intent on the same objective, stopping the Norse invaders before they progressed further into the country.

The morning before, at the market in town, he'd happened on one of the riders sent ahead of the marching army of King Harold. The men were headed for York where a group of invaders led by the king of Norway, the formidable Harold Hardrada, had landed some weeks previously and were creating havoc. The savages had to be stopped at all costs and able-bodied men were asked to join the volunteers already on the move.

Though he himself could be considered, according to Saxons at least, as a "savage", Moon had not hesitated. He would join the expedition. Back at the village, he'd informed his best friend that he would be amongst the men marching on

York. Nothing Torsten had said had dissuaded him. This was the purpose he had been looking for. For months now, he'd been kicking his heels in the village he'd lived in all his life, wondering what to do. At eight and twenty, it was time he did something he could be proud of, and what better than defend the country that had welcomed his Danish father years ago when he'd come in search of peace and acceptance?

Armed with an axe, Moon had left the village in the middle of the night and found the camp of Saxons nestled in the river-bend. As expected, he'd been accepted all too readily, once he had pre-empted all doubts about his intent by addressing them in their language. A man of his stature was a choice recruit.

And so here he was, marching amongst Saxons, about to face warriors many would argue were his own people. This was what came of belonging to two groups, he reflected bitterly, you always had to choose sides. But Moon knew he could not stand by and wait for his country to be torn apart the way it had a long time ago when other groups of Norsemen had spread fear and desolation through it. He was half-Dane, true, but he was also half-Saxon, through his mother Frigyth, and he saw it as his duty to stop anyone trying to harm his people.

For all that, it would be no easy task. There would be the gruesome battle at the end, of course, but even before that, the men were going to be sorely tested. The rigors imposed on the army were relentless, and Moon had to watch as more than one man stumbled. Not long after they had set off that morning, an older man had fallen, never to get back up again. No one had stopped to help, instead doing their best to avoid stomping over him. Indeed, there was no point dragging along a man who would be of no use once they stood in front of Hardrada's army.

No, this was not for the faint-hearted and never had Moon been more grateful for his strong constitution. He could not imagine how someone half his size would fare.

Darkness was already falling when they stopped for the night at the foot of a hill. All around it was a chorus of groans and grunts, soon followed by a few snores. The men were exhausted. Some of them had joined by the south coast and had been marching for longer than a day. Moon unstrapped his axe from his back and stretched. Like the majority of the men, he had to see to his personal needs as a matter as urgency. The opportunity to do so during the day had been non-existent. No sooner had he walked away from the bushes than he was accosted by a rather scruffy man who introduced himself as Farmon.

"Halfdan," Moon replied, nodding in greeting. He rarely used his real name, even when meeting strangers, but if ever there was a time where it was apt, it was now, as it meant "half-Dane."

"I noticed you joined the army this morning, at the same time as me and my friends," the Saxon said, gesturing toward the men standing behind him.

"Yes, I did join this morning."

Whether that was at the same time as them, Moon had no idea, and in all honesty, he didn't care. Farmon, however, didn't pick up on his lack of enthusiasm and carried on explaining that he too had heard the rider calling out to all able-bodied men at the market place.

"As soon as I heard him, I knew I would join the expedition. It seemed the only thing to do. We cannot stand by and watch while our country is ripped to pieces. But I cannot help but wonder at your motives, my friend. What are *you* doing here?" Farmon nodded to him. The meaning of that gesture was clear.

You're not one of us.

As Moon had been fighting with his conscience ever since he'd left the village, he did not take too kindly to the reminder. As a result, he took an instant dislike to the man, even if he knew the question was a fair one. After, all, he did look like a Norseman because, as luck would have it, his mother happened to be blonde and fair as well. In fact, he was the epitome of the giant Norseman Saxons feared, and he towered over Farmon and his friends, a fact he decided to use to his advantage. It wouldn't be the first time he intimidated someone into more respect.

"I was born here, and my mother is a Saxon," he all but growled. "That is precisely why my parents chose to name me Halfdan. It means 'half-Dane', as you might have guessed. And my motives for being here are obvious to me. It is all that matters. They don't have to be obvious to you."

The man raised both hands in surrender, impressed by the ice in his voice as well as his stature, just as expected. "Of course, I'm just saying. Only I saw another Norseman in the ranks earlier. I thought that one joining the army was odd enough, but two..."

Another Norseman? Moon frowned. *Now* he was interested. Who could that other man be? Someone from the village in all probability. But who? Not one of his brothers. He would have known if they had considered joining the army. Not Torsten either, who'd seemed opposed to the idea, despite having an Icelander as a father. So who? His cousins, who had a Saxon mother as well? Curiosity got the better of him. If there was another man with the same dilemma and motives as him in this crowd, it would be worth going to see him. That way they could support each other's decision.

"Do you have any idea where he might be?"

Farmon gestured to a place behind him "Last I saw him he had settled for the night next to the horses, somewhere over there."

"My thanks."

Moon walked over to the place Farmon had indicated and

after a while, spotted a head of blond hair amidst a sea of brown and dark. In the fading light it was shining like a beacon, drawing him in. A Norseman, if he'd ever seen one. He maneuvered to find himself next to the man. Or rather boy, he amended as he got closer. The frame was far too small to be anything else. Unless... The heckles at the back of his neck rose as a horrid thought passed through his mind.

Unless the boy was no boy at all but a reckless, impossibly stubborn female.

He knew someone who fit that description excatly, someone who always got herself involved in scraps and never behaved as she was supposed to. Someone who should be in the village right now, tucked up in bed.

"Eyja?" he called, incredulity making his voice barely audible.

She turned to face him slowly, as if fearing an outburst on his part. Blue eyes, of a blue that had always put him in mind of frost and a full mouth, the color of winter berries. Yes, all that was familiar. It *was* her. But... Her blonde hair, shiny as the sun, had been cut short, much too short, and her slender body was swamped in clothes that had been made for someone twice as big as her.

What the hell?

"Moon." She sounded calm, even if she looked guilty to have been found out.

They stared at each other a long moment. Moon could not fathom how she could be standing next to him. They had been walking all day at punishing speed. If he, with his strong, long legs, had found the march taxing, how had she coped with it? Oh, he knew she was no weakling, but still...

"What are you doing here?" he finally asked in Norse. She would have joined the ranks at the same time as him, during the night. He knew that because he had seen her only the day before, when he'd gone to talk to her brother, Torsten, to tell him about his intentions to join the army, the only person he'd told. So, had she overheard their conversation? Was that what had given her the idea to go and face the Norsemen?

"I heard you talk to Torsten yesterday morning," she answered, confirming his suspicions. He closed his eyes, as guilt and irritation flooded him. How had he not guessed the imp would be spying on them and getting unsuitable ideas? She was always snooping around, always getting herself into all sorts of trouble, as she was proving in spectacular fashion by joining an army of men headed for a massacre. Oblivious to his rising anger, she carried on, as if her bewildering decision could be in any way justified. "I thought what you said about defending our country made sense, and I'm just like you. I, too, was born here, I, too, have a Saxon mother, I, too, want to stop invaders from—"

"But you're *not* just like me, are you!" he roared. Was she really that naïve? "Haven't you forgotten one small detail? Just look at yourself!"

She stiffened under the onslaught. "If you mean that..." Even though they were talking Norse, which no one would understand, she lowered her voice to hiss at him. "If you mean that, unlike you, I'm a woman, then it makes no difference."

By the gods, she really *was* that naïve.

"Does it not?" He crossed his arms over his chest, thereby emphasizing the difference in size between them. She barely reached his shoulder and probably weighed half as much as he did. It did make all the difference, how could she not see it? "Why did you cut off your hair and don men's clothes if you thought you being a woman amidst a sea of men would be of no import? Why didn't you just come in your skirts and long hair?"

She had no answer to that, he was pleased to see.

Doing his best to quell his rising anger, he allowed his eyes to wander over her. The result of his examination was disastrous. She didn't have any weapon that he could see, save for the dagger he knew she always carried in her boot, the blond curls framing her face made her look even more delicate, and the way her clothes swallowed her body was highly suspicious. How in the name of Odin had she ever thought she could pass as a warrior? She looked like a reed amidst a forest of oaks, and just as breakable. What was he to do with her? As if he didn't have enough to worry about, what with him heading for war, now he was saddled with a rash waif!

"And just in case you thought your disguise was a brilliant one, it's not. You look about as believable as a boy as I would as a girl if I put on a dress. Which is to say, not at all," he added before the infuriating woman pointed out that he looked just like his sister Aife. He wouldn't put it past her. She had an unfortunate tendency to be contrary.

Eyja stared at him, appalled. "But I thought..." She ran a hand through her hair and grimaced.

"What? You thought that having short hair was all that was required to be a man?" he huffed. Really, she was naïve beyond belief if she did. "Well, it's not. I have longer hair than most women and yet I don't think anyone would doubt my identity."

The way she swallowed when he straightened to his full height was a small but very real satisfaction. For a moment it looked as if he had the upper hand. Then the maddening woman lifted her chin and looked at him square in the eye.

"Of course I know there is more to being a man than having short hair. But I didn't think anyone would take a peek between my legs. Or are you saying men ogle each other's staff all the time?" she replied, displaying the spirit she was renown for. How had he thought she would ever back off? She never did. He wasn't even sure such a thing was possible. His respect for her increased begrudgingly. Whatever else she was, she was no coward.

"We *don't* ogle one another's staff as a matter of course. And there is no need to take even a glance between your legs to know you're not a man."

She bit her bottom lip, looking crestfallen. "I thought no one would pay enough attention to see anything amiss. After all, why would a woman be here?"

She had a point, not that he would ever admit it. No one would expect to see a woman here, and the men were all too focused on not falling behind to pay too much attention to the others around them. But she was forgetting something.

"Even if that were true and the men didn't notice your frail physique, which I doubt, you look nothing like a Saxon," he said through gritted teeth. "That in itself is enough to attract attention and put you in danger. One of the men was just telling me he'd thought it odd to see Norsemen like us join. Apparently, he's suspicious of our motives. I wouldn't be surprised if he kept a close eye on us."

Her face fell. "Oh. I didn't think of—"

"No, you didn't, did you? Damn it, Imp, your brothers are going to kill me for this!"

Moon buried his axe into the ground in an angry gesture. Eyja would have told no one she was coming, he knew, because if she had even hinted at her intentions, they would have stopped her, and rightly so. This was no place for a vulnerable woman.

"Your father..." He swallowed instead of finishing the sentence. Her father, Wolf, would not only kill him, he would make sure to draw the process out for as long as possible and enjoy every moment of it. No one hurt a member of the Icelander's family and lived to tell the tale. Least of all, his only daughter.

"I will tell them you had no hand in my decision, which is nothing but the truth." Eyja waved his protests away. As if that would be enough, as if it were so simple! She'd always been wild and impulsive, but this was beyond what he had imagined her capable of. Cutting her hair off and dressing herself as a boy, leaving the village without a word, joining an army bound for battle armed only with a dagger. It was extreme, even for her.

"And they will just accept that, will they?" She was even more naïve than he'd thought if she truly believed that. Anyone involved in that disastrous decision of hers would find themselves impacted. He might well have to flee if he survived the battle, because he would face retribution in the village.

Really, what a mess this was.

Just then Farmon drew up next to them. "Ah, I see that you've found the young Norseman. An acquaintance of yours, is he?"

The tilted head made it clear he'd watched the two of them converse and picked up on the connection between them. It would not do to pretend otherwise, as it would only make him more suspicious.

"Yes. As it happens, he's..." Moon did his best to sound natural when referring to Eyja as a man. "My cousin Eirik. We discussed my decision to join the army last night but I had no idea he'd actually come."

He chose his brother's name, which happened to start like her own, in case he forgot to call her by a fake name when taken by surprise. He could always tell everyone that Eyja was a diminutive in Norse for Eirik. The Saxons might not question it. They thought them odd creatures and would accept whatever he told them, if he said it with enough aplomb.

"Your cousin, is he? Well." Farmon arched a brow and looked at one and then the other in quick succession, obviously trying to make sense of the information. "I guess Norsemen come in all shapes and sizes, even in families. Let us hope the ones we are about to face take more after young Eirik than you."

The man to his right sniggered. "If they do, they won't know what hit them."

"Aye, we'll quickly make them regret their decision to come over here and steal what's ours."

The Saxons were still laughing when they made their way to the river to have a drink. Moon turned back to face Eyja. She hadn't uttered a single word during the exchange with the men, which had surprised him. It had been the wisest thing to do, undoubtedly, but she wasn't exactly renowned for her patience. He'd lost count of the amount of times she'd been unable to hold her tongue when the situation demanded it.

As if to prove he was right to marvel at her unusual compliance, she glared at him and launched her attack.

"So, I'm your cousin, am I?"

She didn't seem best pleased by the lie. But what did she expect? That he would wash his hands off of her and let her face the men on her own? He would not. Even if he had not asked for her presence, he could not abandon her now.

"Yes, you are until I say differently," he snapped. Naming her as his cousin would ensure the men knew that she—*he*—was under his protection. It was the best he could do. "You are not to leave my side for a moment, do you hear? Make sure you talk as little as possible, and try to modify your voice when you do. Better yet, just leave and go back home while you still can."

"I'm not leaving," she instantly answered, as he'd known she would. Why was he even bothering? She would never agree to be ordered about.

In any case, and even if he would never tell her as much, he didn't really like the idea of her being alone on the roads. Without a mounted king urging her on, she wouldn't walk anywhere near as fast as they had done today so the journey back would take her two whole days. It wasn't safe for a woman to be on her own for so long.

But her staying here was no solution either. They were going to war, damn it, not to pick mushrooms!

"Fine. Stay then," he said between his teeth. "But do as I say, or so help me, I will become your worst nightmare."

For the sake of everyone around them, Moon worked hard at maintaining a calm surface but deep down, he was furious.

The imp had really gone and done it this time.

SITTING in the grass next to Moon, Eyja did not know how to feel.

Part of her was annoyed to have been found out so quickly. That had not been the plan. She had intended to pass unnoticed, which should have been easy in this crowd. Since Moon towered above the others, it was not difficult to spot where he was and avoid him. All day long she had stayed well behind, hidden in the throng of men, in the hope he wouldn't know she was here, because there was no prize guessing he would not approve of her joining the army. But her luck hadn't held out. As soon as they had stopped for the night, he'd seen her. Just as she had imagined, he did not seem best pleased to have been saddled with her. However, it was clear that he felt it his responsibility to stay with her. She would not be allowed, or able, to shake him off.

Eyja did not look forward to having to endure his foul mood for days on end.

Another, bigger part of part of her, was relieved not to be alone anymore. The day had been horrid, much more than she had anticipated. The grueling pace imposed on the men, she had fully expected, but it didn't mean it had been easy to cope with. Her feet were burning, her legs felt as weak as distended ropes. King Harold was bent on surprising the Norsemen before they could regroup and organize themselves and was marching his recruits on relentlessly. As a consequence, she had seen more than one man left behind by the side of the road. No, she had guessed the march would tax her strength to the limit.

But what had been much worse was the way they had all ogled her, made her feel like an oddity and a stranger. Because of the way she looked with her blond hair and blue eyes, they had been suspicious of her origins. That had been bad enough, but on more than one occasion she had caught a questioning look on a man's face. Thanks to Moon's comment, she now knew that they had been wondering if aught was amiss. They had been questioning her motives as well as her physique.

Fortunately, everyone's focus had been on putting one foot in front of the other as quickly as possible and she had been able to melt into the crowd before questions could be asked.

But now they had stopped and she could feel dozens of eyes on her, which was why she was grateful for Moon's presence by her side. Before she could think, she wiggled closer to him. Never had she had more cause to appreciate his bulk and strength. People would think twice about bothering him or his "cousin".

"Tell me what I can do to pass off as a man," she whispered in his ear. Now that she had been found out, she might as well make the most of his help.

"You can't," was his irritated answer. "Everything about you is wrong. You're too small, too delicate, you move like a woman, you sound like a woman, you smell like a woman, you even eat like a woman."

He nodded at the piece of bread she was holding, as if to prove his point. She frowned, looking at her fingers. What could he possibly mean? "How do you mean?"

"Where did you find those clothes anyway?" he added instead of offering explanation as to what she was doing wrong.

"They're too big for you, another reason why you look all wrong. How many people have you seen wear clothes that were not made for them?"

She hesitated, knowing he would hate her answer. But there had been no choice. Her brothers were far too big for her to even think of using their clothes.

"After I heard you and Torsten talk, I saw Hilda had placed some clothes by the riverbank to dry. I took them," she finally admitted. The woman's son Ari was sixteen yet apparently bigger and stronger than her, judging from the way the shirt and braies fit her. But there had been no time to take them in and anyway, having spend her childhood running after boys in the forest, she was not really skilled with the needle. She was much more at home with snares.

"So you mean you stole them?" As predicted, Moon was not impressed.

Eyja felt herself go red to the roots of her hair. A bad idea. Moon would tell her she blushed like a woman, no doubt. Thankfully, it was now full dark so he might not see. Still, for more safety, she lowered her head. "It's not stealing. I fully intend to give them back when I return."

"Mm. But will he want them with a dozen slashes and holes in them? That's the question." This time she knew she had blanched. Moon let out a little irritated noise at her reaction. "Bloody hell, Eyja, what do you expect will happen once we're facing the Norsemen? That they will take one look at us and run like startled coneys? They will fight us, and what's worse, they will fight to the death. They are skilled, determined warriors."

He was right. This was no game. A good number of the men around them would be dead in a couple of days time, and they would have died a horrible death.

She stared at Moon, as the reality of the situation sank in. They were going to war.

They might never come back.

"Yes, they are," she whispered.

If he heard the consternation in her voice, he chose to ignore it. "Which brings me to your dagger."

"My dagger?"

He nodded toward her left leg. "I expect you are carrying it in your boot as you always do? Well, what do you expect to do with it? Cut your cheese into neat little cubes, like only a woman would do?" He sounded so irate that she recoiled. They'd had their disagreements over the years but he had never spoken to her so scathingly before and she didn't know how to deal with it. "This is war. You need a real weapon, not something that belongs in a kitchen. Why didn't you take your father's sword? It's the best one in the village."

"I... I thought about it but I can't wield it."

He groaned at her admission. "Of course you can't, because—"

He did not finish the sentence. There was no need. *Because you're a woman.*

Everything collapsed within Eyja. Yes, she *was* a woman, armed with only a small dagger, a woman who had never fought or even slapped anyone in her life, who had no idea what she was doing. For the first time, the enormity of what she was about to face struck her. What was she doing here? She would not last a moment against the Norse warriors, most of them she expected to be Berserkers. She had heard her father and his friends talk about the half-crazed warriors enough times to know they could not be disposed of like ordinary men. Once the killing frenzy had seized them, they were virtually invincible and fought to the death.

Though her appetite had quite deserted her, she forced herself to finish the last piece of bread she'd been handed by one of the king's men. She would need all her strength in the days to come.

"I'm tired," she said once she had finally managed to swallow the mouthful of hard dough. "I'd better get some sleep while I can, and hope I do not look like a woman when I sleep."

"Good luck with that, because you do," was all the answer she got.

CHAPTER TWO

The next day was just as grueling as the previous one had been, and the unseasonably hot weather didn't help, nor did the lack of opportunities to drink or eat. The men didn't have time for anything else other than to forge ahead. Personal needs, along with any doubts they might have, had best be forgotten or ignored.

It was exhausting, but it did have one advantage.

Eyja had feared having to answer Moon's questions or try to justify her decision not to heed his advice about heading back home but they barely talked as they walked side by side. Every breath was precious. In those circumstances, arguing was not only pointless, but also potentially dangerous. By the time the halt was called, Eyja could barely see. When she fell to her knees with a groan she expected Moon to mock her, or at the very least point out that she would not last another day.

But to her surprise, he didn't pass any comment and just sat down next to her. His anger seemed to have vanished. It was as if he'd walked it out during the day, or come to the conclusion that he had better accept the fact that she was here because he could not change it. She was grateful for it, as the last thing she needed right now was a remonstrance. She lay on the ground motionless a long moment, staring at the darkening sky. In what state would she arrive in York? She didn't know how to fight, and that was worrying enough, but she was now wondering if she would even have the strength to stand there while the Norsemen charged at her.

Shouldn't she go back?

No. Not now.

She would push on and pretend she was all right, just like she had always done in times of difficulty.

"I should have taken our gelding." Moon was eyeing up the group of horses grazing in the distance. Some of the men, including, of course, the king and all his courtiers, were mounted. Unsurprisingly, they were having an easier time than the rest of them. "At least you would have been able to travel in more comfort."

"I will be just fine," Eyja said, cheered by the idea that he was worried about her. It was much better than being angry. She should have guessed his anger would not last. Moon had always been reasonable and fair. He often ranted when she joined the boys' expeditions, but ultimately, he always agreed to let her tag along. That was one of the things she liked best about him, he accepted her for who she was, and never suggested she change. Some of her brothers' friends were less generous. "And if you'd have brought your horse, *you* would have ridden him, not me."

"As if I would have let you gainsay me," he huffed, confident in his physical superiority. "I would have sat your ass on the horse and that would have been that."

"You're forgetting that I can jump! I was never going to just meekly sit there, you know. Or did you plan to tie my legs together at the ankles under his belly? I wouldn't put it past you, you brute."

He glowered at her but did not answer. She didn't insist. It was not worth carrying on this discussion when they were both as stubborn as each other. But she was glad to be able to bicker with him. It was not quite peace, but the kind of teasing they had always enjoyed, and much better than any argument.

"Wait here, I'll be right back," he said once they'd been handed a meager portion of dried meat and bread to eat. It was hardly what she would call tasty but there was little point in complaining or even pointing it out. There would not be anything else.

Chewing on the tough piece of beef, she watched Moon walk toward the left of the camp. Most probably, he was going to see to his needs. This was one of the reasons she was most glad of his presence. He guarded her privacy when she squatted behind a bush, as, of course, she could not do like the other men while on the go, and simply stop by the side of the road to relieve herself. He had made her go as they were slowing down for the night, taking advantage of a clump of trees conveniently situated.

After having been by Moon's side all day Eyja felt vulnerable without him, like a warrior removing his armor might feel. She ate, doing her best to chew like a man and not meet anyone's eye.

Soon he was back with an axe in hand.

"What's that?"

"*That* is an axe." He sat down and placed it next to his own.

"Well. Yes. I can see that."

He shrugged apologetically. "You asked."

"I meant... You know very well what I meant!"

"Do I? I've never been able to make heads or tails of what goes on in that mind of yours. You did once think it a good idea to include ants in your mother's pottage, remember? Who else would have thought that a tasty addition? Not your parents or your brothers, if I remember correctly, and I can't say I blame them."

He bit into his piece of bread to hide a smirk. Eyja felt her lips quiver. How was he doing this? She was exhausted, hungry, scared, and yet somehow he managed to make her laugh.

"Very well. Where did you find the axe and why is it here?" There, the question could not be clearer. He would have no choice but to answer.

"I told you. You need a proper weapon. This one is for you."

"Who gave it to you?" Surely whoever had brought it along would not want to face the Norsemen unarmed?

"No one gave it to me. I swapped it for my belt buckle."

"The one Caedmon made for you?" She was incredulous. The exquisite silver piece had to be worth a dozen axes at the very least, and he had squandered it away on a perfectly ordinary weapon,

Moon only shrugged. "He can make me another when I come back. It's not going to be of any use to me in battle. But we do need an axe."

We. That simple word reduced her insides to mush. He was looking after her, providing her with what she needed when she'd thought he would be furious. But it turned out that instead of finding ways to send her back home, he had spent the day plotting a way to get her a proper weapon. She could have cried.

"Who did you get it from?" she asked instead.

"I saw a man laden with blades of all kinds ahead of us while we marched. I went to him, argued that he only had two hands, and could not wield all of them at once, but he might want to have something to sell once the battle was over, to ensure himself a proper celebration. He agreed."

This didn't surprise her. Moon could talk anyone into anything when the mood took him. She had once seen him convince a Danish merchant to take a trunk filled with presents on board his ship to be delivered to Eowyn, a Saxon friend of his mother's who had moved to Denmark after marrying a Dane. Though the trunk was heavy and cumbersome, the man had agreed not only to transport it, but to bring it to Eowyn and her husband Rune's home. Yes, Moon could get any man to do his bidding. As for women, it was even worse, he didn't even have to talk. A smile and a wink were usually enough to win them around. She had seen it often enough.

Reassured by the sight of the blade, she lay back down. At least now she was properly armed.

"Oh, and just so we're clear, I will be carrying the axe while we walk," he added. "It's a bit heavy for a..." He stopped before he could say the word "woman" and ruin the new peace between them. Eyja barely repressed a smile, enjoying their restored complicity.

"For a...?" she challenged, curious to see how he would finish that sentence.

"For a youth who hasn't yet sprouted hair on his chin."

"Mm. Yes." Relieved to know she wouldn't have to carry the cumbersome weapon, she didn't insist. It was bad enough walking with a dagger in her boot. "Thank you, Moon. I don't know what to say."

"Well. That would be a first." He snorted and then planted his gaze into hers. In the silvery light, he looked unusually earnest. "Don't say anything then. Just make sure you use it well when the time comes, all right?"

THE THIRD MORNING was much the same as the two previous ones but the crossing of a river proved to be more problematic than the king and his men had anticipated and slowed them down, forcing the men to take a well-earned rest. More and more people were joining them all the time. Thanks to the riders sent ahead, word that they were recruiting was spreading fast and there were lots of volunteers who wanted to fight the invaders.

When they stopped that night, Moon was pleased to see that, thanks to the unplanned rest, Eyja appeared less exhausted than she had the previous two evenings. In truth, he was impressed by her resilience. Where did the girl put her grit and determination? It was no surprise that someone like him should be able to endure the relentless pace, but her? There was nothing of her. Physically, at least. Her mind, however, was forged of the strongest steel. He'd always known she had a strong will but to see it proven so unequivocally was humbling. There seemed to be little merit for a strong man like him to join such an enterprise, but for a woman who'd never wielded a weapon or even slapped someone in her life, it was a daunting prospect to say the least.

And yet here she was, doggedly making her way, ensuring she didn't fall behind. The only concession she had allowed was to let him carry the axe he'd procured for her. To his surprise, he enjoyed having her by his side even if they didn't talk much. Today, though, thanks to the delay at the bridge, they had been able to do something other than watch where to put their feet and he had made the most of it to get to know her better.

Usually when she was around—and she nearly always was —he talked to her brothers, not her. She was part of a group but never at the center of it and he did little more than tease her. Now that she was the sole focus of his attention, he discovered an unsuspected side to her. She was easy to be with, had a ready sense of humor and was surprisingly knowledgeable on a variety of subjects, as well as brave and loyal.

Talking to her in Norse amongst people who didn't under-stand what they were saying made their connection even more special and he found himself rather... well, entranced by her, a most unexpected development.

After another frugal meal of bread and hard cheese, they lay next to one another, just as they had done the two previous nights. High above, a crescent of moon illuminated the night sky. Against his back, the mossy ground was soft and welcoming. Around them, the exhausted army was falling asleep. In just a few days the whole thing had acquired a kind of regularity that was almost soothing. Odd how one could so quickly adapt to a new reality and find it satisfying. Moon closed his eyes. They were getting closer and closer to their goal, and would need to be at their best to have a chance at survival.

Just as he was about to drop off, he heard Eyja's voice, soft and dreamy in his ear.

"Moon."

"Mm?"

"What do you think your parents would call you if you did not have a mark in the shape of a moon on your wrist?"

"I don't know." He uncovered the purple mark stamped on the inside of his left wrist. It was about the size of a coin. Part of a coin to be exact, a crescent, the same shape as the one shining over them at that moment. That was probably what had put Eyja in mind of it. He tapped his finger lightly over it. "I've never asked myself that question. They would simply use my name, Halfdan, I suppose."

"It would have been a pity. Moon suits you."

"Well, you say that now, but if my mark had been shaped like a line and they had called me Worm, you would have agreed it was the perfect name for me."

She giggled, a sound he should have remonstrated her for, as it sounded nothing like what his "cousin" Eirik should sound. But he didn't have the heart to. It impressed him that, in spite of everything, she still had enough spirit to laugh. "No. Not Worm. Snake at the very least. You're too massive to be a worm."

"I'm sure that's meant to be a compliment, so thank you."

There was laughter in her voice when she answered. "Not a compliment, just a fact."

"Mm. Thanks anyway."

She took hold of his wrist to peer at it. Moon found himself watching the way her fingers could not close around it. For a reason he could not explain, it caused him to swallow. Something was different between them tonight. Was it due to the time they had spent this afternoon, joking and getting to know one another better? He didn't know, but one thing was certain, only the night before he would not have registered the softness of her fingers on his skin or been unsettled by the proof that she was as feminine as he was masculine.

"I wish I had a mark like yours. It's always fascinated me. When I was young, one day I drew some on my whole body with charcoal. Moons and suns and stars and various animals." He felt her shrug. "I wanted to be like you. My mother went mad when she had to scrub me raw that night."

"Again," he couldn't help but add. With a daughter like Eyja, forever getting into scraps, Merewen would have had her hands full.

She giggled. "Yes, again. I've lost count of the times she had to wash me from head to toe."

A light finger landed on his skin, and Eyja started to idly trace the contours of the mark. Everything within him tensed. The caress—for it felt like a caress, even if she had not intended it to be—was creating very disturbing sensations within him.

He took his arm away with a frown. "Stop that."

"Oh, you're ticklish then? How come I never knew that?" Eyja sounded utterly delighted, only adding to his discomfort.

"I'm not," he said through gritted teeth." He was... aroused, that was what he was. The realization was as unwelcome as a slap. His best friend's sister, a woman he had known all her life, was getting his blood up with her sensual touch. How was he supposed to handle that notion?

"Are you sure you're not ticklish? Let's see."

With those words, the minx fell on him. For a moment he was too stunned by the feel of a supple, feminine body atop his to react as he should. Her hands bracketed his body, her breasts —yes, she *had* breasts, apparently, how come he had never really noticed before?—pressed against his chest, her scent wrapped around him. He closed his eyes when her thigh rubbed against his groin, awakening sensations that should not have been awakened by her.

Everything within him leapt in protest.

This was wrong.

It was Eyja on top of him, not a conquest ripe for the taking. He could not lose sight of that fact.

"Enough!" he hissed, pining her in place next to him. "Bloody hell, you can be such a child sometimes. You wanted to be a man, well, act like one! Men do not giggle, they do not tickle each other, and cousins certainly do not caress each other's wrists, do you hear, they do not lie on top of each other. You really are irresponsible. Do you want everyone here to think us lovers? Stop touching me, stop teasing me, stop... plain annoying me! Don't you think you have done enough already?"

Her eyes became two huge, glittering pools and he instantly regretted his harshness. It was not her fault he had momentarily forgotten where and who they were, and felt fleeting, painful desire toward her. In fact she would probably be horrified if she knew.

Eyja's insides withered under the violence of the attack.

Never had she seen Moon so furious. His body, so close to hers, was radiating fury, his face was contorted in a feral grimace.

But still she didn't try to fight the hold pinning her in place or protest, because he was right. She had wanted to pass herself off as a man, and men did not cry. Warriors on campaign did not sob like women, so she would not either.

But it cost her all her inner strength not to.

Stop plain annoying me. Haven't you done enough already?

The words twisted her guts. That he wanted to protect her and keep her real identity a secret was one thing, but this was different. He wanted her to stop being a burden for him.

"I understand," she said, her voice a deathly whisper. "I won't bother you again."

There was a silence, as if Moon was pondering on the best way to answer. Then finally he let go of her wrists and turned his back to her.

"Good." That one word sounded like a condemnation. "Now go to sleep."

Sleep? Incredulity made her blink. Did he really think she would be able to sleep after what had happened? Her chest was aching as badly as if he'd physically punched her. Never had he spoken to her in that way before. Even when he'd been angry that she had followed him in this expedition, it had not hurt as much. That evening he had criticized her decision, something anyone with sense would have done. After all, she had placed herself into a dangerous, potentially lethal situation. But this time it was different, this time it was personal. He'd called her an irresponsible child, he'd asked her to stop annoying him. She wasn't sure how to recover from such a blow to her feelings.

But it was not just the pain of his last words that prevented her from slipping into oblivion.

It was an odd restlessness in her lower body.

Feeling his hard chest under her when she'd tried to tickle him, his hands around her wrists when he had pinned her in place, his breath against her neck when he'd talked to her, had caused something inside her to shift. For a moment they had been in a very provocative position and her whole body had leapt in approval, almost in recognition, as if that was what it had hankered for all along. Perhaps it had.

Moon had never seen her like a woman, but she had been aware he was a man for years, ever since she had stopped being a child herself. Because of his lack of interest in her, however, she'd had to resign herself and pretend she agreed that nothing could happen between them.

But tonight... Something different had happened. The old Moon would simply have laughed when she'd started to tickle him, thrown her to one side and mocked her weakness, or tickled her back and shown her who was stronger. Instead, he'd kept her on top of him for longer than necessary and held her tight against his chest, his fingers splayed around her waist in a way she could only call sensual.

And she'd felt...

Heat invaded her cheeks. She'd felt him harden against her. It had been unmistakable. She knew all too well this was what happened when men got aroused. Say what he might, he had been affected as much as she had been. Obviously, their provocative position was responsible for this unexpected development, not her per se, but all the same, he had been aroused by her proximity and his arousal had provoked hers in turn. It was hard to be writhing atop a man such as Moon and remain indifferent.

What could she do now? Nothing. She could not slip a hand between her legs and ease the need he'd fired inside her, not here out in the open, not while she was wearing braies, not in the middle of thousands of men, not when there was a risk Moon would see her and know what their tussle had done to her.

There was only one thing to do.

Sleep, just as he'd said, and leave him alone.

CHAPTER THREE

E ven before he opened his eyes, Moon knew something was wrong.

Eyja was not by his side. He felt her absence in his bones, with as much certainty as he would have known without moving that someone had removed his boots or shaved his head during the night. The sensation was imperceptible and yet undeniable.

He opened his eyes. Dawn had not even broken yet. Where was she? Had she gone to see to her needs upon waking up? It was always a delicate moment, as she could not relieve herself out in the open like the other men, so usually he kept watch when she needed privacy. Had the imp decided to let him sleep a while longer and risk doing it all on her own?

No. It was much worse than that.

It all came back to him in a rush. Their unexpected moment of intimacy the night before, when she had stroked his wrist and caused his blood to surge, their tussle and tumble afterward when she had tried to tickle him, their argument when he had snarled at her for doing nothing more than being herself.

Her promise never to bother him again.

Blood froze in his veins.

Where was she? Surely she hadn't left the army, gone back home all alone now that they were so close to their destination? No. In all likelihood she would be hiding amongst the men. He bolted to his feet, determined to find her before the army marched on, or at least try to. If she'd gone to the other side of the camp while he slept, oblivious to it all, he might never find her. There were just too many people. Bloody hell, would there be no end to the worry she gave him?

For a long moment, he wandered around the waking men, looking for a blonde, delicate head. He even asked a few people if they had seen his "cousin". But no one could or wanted to help him. The men had other priorities than looking for an elusive boy at the moment.

And then he saw it.

A few yards away two men were kicking at a third one. A slender, vulnerable one.

"Wake up, sleepyhead! It's time to leave. Where do you think you are?"

Moon arrived in time to stop one of the Saxons from grabbing Eyja by the collar. "Leave h...im alone!" he snarled, remembering just in time to refer to her as a boy. He placed himself between her and her attacker, much as a dog would when defending its master. A growling watch dog, was that what he was reduced to now? The worst of it was, he did not even mind.

"Where does the lad think he is?" the man spat. "At home suckling his mother's teats? We're on a march, in case you hadn't noticed!"

"I had noticed, thank you. That's why he's exhausted."

That was no lie at least. The purple shadows on Eyja's cheeks bore witness to her fatigue, while the red rims around her eyes told him that she had cried herself to sleep the night before. Because of him.

His chest tightened in guilt. Why had he been so harsh with her?

The only explanation he could think of was that he had been thrown off guard by what had happened between them. The feel of his wrist imprisoned in her small, delicate fingers, the sensuality of the caress on his skin, the weight of her over him, the way she had writhed and rubbed against him... It had all been too much. Or not enough. Or... Something.

For the first time last night he had realized that, even if he had never treated her as such during their childhood, Eyja was a woman, and a beautiful one. For the first time she had *felt* like a woman against him, and he had not been able to deal with it. The irony of the situation was not lost on him and did little to help him make sense of it all.

As a young boy, he had never thought of her as a girl. Later, when he'd grown, she'd never been someone he considered bedding. Not only was she seven years younger than him, little more than a child in his eyes, but she was his friends' sister, and therefore out of bounds. Despite their frequent dips in the river when he had glimpsed her form clad only in wet garments, he had never been attracted to her in that way. She had simply been part of the group, yet someone else to frolic with. But since she had cut her hair and donned men's clothes, all he could see was her feminine grace. Perhaps the coarse, slightly too loose clothes emphasized the slenderness of her body, perhaps the harsh haircut drew attention to her fine features.

He didn't know what it was but all of a sudden she was unequivocally, worryingly alluring.

It was lucky the men were too focused on a single objective and too tired to look twice at each other or they would have seen her for who she truly was. It seemed to Moon that no woman had ever been more feminine. His body at least wasn't fooled, and last night it had manifested its approval.

"We're not so exhausted that we cannot give you savages a taste of our Saxon pluck," the man in front of him growled, nodding at his menacing friend who growled in turn. "It would be good practice for when we face Hardrada's men, I'd say."

Moon tensed. The situation was deteriorating rapidly. He felt Eyja shuffle closer to him, as if she wanted to disappear behind his bulk. Too late. The damage had already been done. Other men had started to draw closer. Moon could have handled two men on his own, but not two dozen. Just as he was wondering if he had not better tackle the two brutes now, before the vultures decided that they, too, wanted a taste of the Norsemen, a voice spoke from behind him.

"Leave them be. The king needs every man he can get in his army. He will not be best pleased to see us put each other out of action before we even reach York." It was Farmon, the man from his town, surrounded by his group of friends. The situation was turned on its head and the two Saxons were suddenly the ones outnumbered two to one. "And if the lad's tired, then it's no wonder, given his frail constitution. The fact that he is still here in spite of it proves his courage."

After a last grumble, the two thugs went their way and the rest of the men returned to their business without a comment.

"Thank you," Moon told Farmon. His intervention had been timely, there was no denying it. Had he misjudged the man? Perhaps. After all, nothing had forced him to intervene in their favor.

The Saxon nodded, as if he didn't need to be thanked for doing what was only right. "No problem. As I said, it's in our best interest to reach Hardrada's army hale and hardy."

"Of course. Still."

Eyja was still hovering behind him, not showing herself.

This subdued attitude worried him. She had not said a word since he'd found her or even thanked Farmon for his help.

Before he knew what he was doing, Moon turned around to face her.

"Listen, I'm sorry about last night."

The words took him by surprise. He'd meant to berate her for leaving his side and exposing herself to danger and here he was, apologizing to her instead. But she didn't even acknowledge it, simply lowered her head and waited. This proved more clearly than anything else that something had changed between them. Only the day before she would have jumped at the chance to goad him about apologizing unprompted, something he rarely found within himself to do. How could he make her see he truly was sorry for hurting her?

Before he could come up with a solution, the signal for departure was rung. The men grunted and started to gather their weapons. A moment later, they were off.

It was a while before Moon picked up the courage to speak again. Eyja was walking beside him, as she had done for the last three days, but he could feel how heavy her steps were, and there was a defeated slant to her shoulders. She certainly was nothing like the stubborn, assertive imp he knew. That girl would have sent him to Hell and Helheim. The one currently walking next to him was both subdued and afraid. He hated it. It was unnatural, and, worst of all, it was all his fault. He felt like a man who had uprooted a wild medlar tree at the height of its blooming magnificence to plant it in front of his hut for practicality's sake, only to have to watch it wither away in its new unsuitable environment.

No more sweet fruits for him.

No more peevish comments either.

"Eyja. Please, talk to me."

Silence. He didn't know whether to insist or not. Had he not wreaked enough damage? Then, to his relief, she spoke.

"It's all right. There's no need for you to apologize or say anything. You were right last night." Every short sentence was punctuated by a few sluggish strides and her voice was painfully flat, nothing like her usual tones. "It's time I started acting like a man."

No.

The word leapt to his throat and he almost let it slip out of his lips. Why should she act like someone she was not? Why should she pretend to be a warrior when she was just as brave, just as reliable as any of the men around them anyway? It didn't seem fair.

"I shouldn't have said what I said, it was mean. I only meant—"

"Forget it. As I said, you were right. I came here dressed as a boy so as to pass unnoticed and against all odds, it worked. Now is not the time to give away my real identity by foolish actions."

Eyja didn't want Moon to feel guilty and, even more importantly, she didn't want any misunderstanding to linger between them on the eve of battle. Tomorrow they might both be dead. She didn't want their last words to each other to be bitter ones.

Last words. Dear, that sounded so awful she almost collapsed.

She bunched her fists, as if that would be enough to strengthen her resolve. "Tonight we'll probably reach York. Tomorrow or the day after at the latest, we will face the invaders and do what we came here to do. We will fight, and perhaps we will die." She could barely speak for the tightening in her throat and the fear in her gut. "I've known you all my life and I don't want us to part as enemies over something so stupid as the best moment to tickle somebody."

There was a brush against her shoulder. The innocuous

gesture would not have attracted anyone's attention but she knew it had been deliberate. She closed her eyes briefly, relishing it.

"We will never be enemies. You need not fear that. And I am sorry for what I said, Imp."

The use of the familiar nickname as well as the earnestness in his voice made her defenses crumble and, this time, she did trip. Moon caught her elbow as easily as if he'd expected her to falter and had been ready to catch her. Then he gave it a light squeeze, the gesture of support unmistakable, the meaning behind it, clear.

Men don't embrace each other, otherwise I would draw you into my arms right now.

A tear threatened to escape her eyes and this proof of weakness made her bristle. She knew when she brushed it away that Moon would not berate her but still it was not wise to let anyone else see. They were surrounded by men whose tempers were starting to fray, it would not take much to push one or more over the edge, she had seen it that morning.

Had Farmon not intervened, things could have taken a nasty turn.

She had been surprised to see him offer up his help and she was grateful for it, but all things considered she would have preferred him and his men to stop hovering around them. The less interest people took in her, the more chance she had of keeping her identity a secret. But it seemed that the scruffy Saxon and his friends could not get past the fact that she and Moon were half-Norse. Was that the reason for their constant presence around them? Were they keeping an eye on them, thinking them traitors who would give the army the slip and run ahead to warn Hardrada about the upcoming attack when they got nearer to York? He would not expect King Harold, who had been all the way down south when the invaders' ships had landed, to arrive for another few days. This was the whole point of this forced march.

The Saxons were counting on surprise to give them an edge over their enemies.

If Farmon was convinced they were spies intent on warning the Norse king an attack was coming, he would not leave them out of his sight. Eyja had better be on her guard and ensure she did not betray her real identity by an inconsiderate gesture or comment.

They walked on, the prospect of soon being at their destination lending new energy to the men. After a while she heard Moon's voice, gruffer than usual. "I'm proud of you, Eyja. I want you to know that."

Everything within her melted. She could hear he meant it absolutely and it was the best compliment he could have given her.

"Please don't," she whispered. "Not now, not when I'm already doing all I can not to cry."

"I know. That's one of the reasons I'm so proud of you."

He turned his head to look at her. With the two axes strapped to his back, the determination etched on his face, and the muscles rippling under his tunic, he looked every inch the formidable warrior. She should have been terrified. She was instead comforted. With this man by her side, nothing bad could happen to her. They were friends, no matter what. He would not let her down.

"Thank you. I'm proud of you too."

He snorted, just as she expected. "You're a veritable imp, you know that?"

"I do."

Finally, as the sun started to lower toward the horizon, they arrived in view of the town of York, their final destination. They had completed the journey in record time and were ready for the long-awaited confrontation.

As she lay down on the ground that night, Eyja was thankful for her state of exhaustion. Perhaps it would allow her to get the rest she needed, because without it she might well have worked herself up into a panic at the thought of what was to come.

Tomorrow they would face Harald Hardrada's formidable army.

CHAPTER FOUR

The roar rising from the other side of the river caused Eyja's insides to liquefy with fear. This was it. After all the wait and anticipation, the exhausting march, the last preparations at dawn, the moment to fight had finally come.

All the air left her lungs and she tightened her fist around the axe Moon had found for her. Despite the fearsome weapon, she felt woefully vulnerable. She did not imagine how she would be feeling right now if she'd only had her small dagger to hang on to. Thanks be to the gods for his foresight and generosity.

"Looks like we'll have an easy time of it," the man next to her observed under his breath. "I hadn't dared hope for such favorable conditions."

Even if she wasn't convinced it would be that simple, Eyja knew what he meant. The king's plan had worked, and the invaders army had clearly been taken by surprise by their swift arrival. As a result, they were scattered about, and would not be able to regroup in time to face their attackers as one. King Harold had been informed that morning that a good portion of the Norse army was stationed further away, too far to be of any use at the moment. Not only that, but due to the hot weather, they had not donned their chainmail. As the majority of the Saxons weren't equipped either, it meant they were on a more equal footing.

Still, that did not, despite what the man thought, make it quite "easy" for them, and the unseasonably warm weather was not responsible for the sweat running down her back. The warriors facing them from across the water looked formidable, more than she had feared.

She stole a glance in Moon's direction. Like everyone else, he was staring at the other side of the river, where an odd spectacle was playing out.

King Harold had gone to speak to his brother, Tostig, who had betrayed him and got in league with Hardrada. The confrontation between the two brothers would be tense, and Eyja wasn't sure what could be accomplished. Was the king really hoping the invaders would turn around and leave just because he was asking?

Moon seemed to read her mind and leaned in to speak in her ear. "He will be offering his brother the chance to betray the Norse king, no doubt, and save his skin. In exchange for his allegiance and his men's help in the fight, his life will be spared," he said, nodding to the men on horseback in the middle of the clearing.

The way they interacted seemed to make sense to him. It didn't to her. "Do you really think Tostig will agree to it?" Hope surged through her. Could they avoid a massacre?

"I don't think so, not without strong guarantees, at least. Look at the way he sits on his horse."

Indeed, the Saxon's attitude was not promising. The discussion was not going well, and Hardrada, who presumably didn't understand a word of it, was starting to get impatient. *He* didn't seem open to any negotiations and was itching to get this over with. He shouted something at the two brothers, his voice carrying through the air with the sureness of an arrow, but he was too far away for Eyja to understand what he had said.

A moment later King Harold rode back toward his army, looking grim, and Tostig joined Hardrada's side. There was only one conclusion to be drawn from this.

The parley had failed. Now battle was inevitable.

Eyja swallowed as battle cries started to erupt around them. The slim hope she had held on to against all reason was shattered. Was she the only one to deplore the failure of the negotiations? Apparently so. The men seemed raring to go.

"Moon, I'm... scared."

It was not easy to utter the words. Never before had she admitted to such a thing. Growing up in a group of boys, it had been essential never to betray any weakness and keep her doubts to herself, or they would never have allowed her to stay with them. But if ever an occasion warranted honesty, this was it.

Moon grunted, as if she'd said nothing out of the ordinary. "Of course, you are, anyone in their right mind would be scared right now."

The sheer bluntness of the statement was comforting. He was not trying to hide his feelings, or posing as a seasoned warrior immune to fear and doubt, he was not impressing over her, a mere woman, the fact that men did not tremble before battle.

"Stay next to me while we fight," he instructed, his gaze never leaving the sea of heads on the other side of the river.

She didn't answer. What would be the point of promising such a thing when they both knew it would be impossible for them to remain side by side in the thick of the battle? They would have a hard enough time trying to stay alive.

Finally, he glanced at her. In the morning sunshine his eyes were piercing blue, his hair shiny as gold. He looked both familiar and out of place. Around them the other men had brown hair as short as she had, and no beards.

A terrifying though tore through her.

Would he not be mistaken for one of the enemies when the fighting started and men started to mingle? No one looked more like a Norseman than Moon. Some of the Saxons were aware of him, and knew he was on their side, but not everyone in the vast army did. In the heat of the battle, he might well become a target for their blows. On the other hand, and for the same reason, the men from Hardrada's army might leave him alone when they mistook him for one of their own. Ironically, he might well find himself fending off his countrymen's attacks rather than fighting the invaders he had come to meet.

She didn't have the same issue. She was blonde, true, but so were some other Saxons, and she didn't have a beard or long, braided hair that marked her out as Norse. She would not be mistaken for anything other than a puny Saxon who should have stayed at home.

"You look like—"

"I know." From the way he interrupted her, Eyja understood he had reached the same conclusion as she had. "It doesn't matter."

"No." She didn't know what else to answer. Her mind had gone blank, her body liquid with fear. How on earth was she going to survive this? Her legs were barely able to support her. As soon as they started to run she might well trip and be trampled by the charging Saxons, long before she had time to raise her axe. What a waste that would be.

"It's not too late to run, you know." Moon glanced behind them, to the clump of bushes beckoning a short distance away.

"While everyone's attention is on the fight ahead, you could reach the—"

"No." It was not an option. "I'm not leaving. I'm not leaving you."

"Imp—"

"Please, Moon."

Though he had called her this all her life, right now hearing the word wanted to make her cry. She could not bear it, not when it was costing her all her willpower not to crumple.

Around them things had descended into utter chaos. The order to attack had been given and the army was trying to breach the bridge, which was the only way to get the other side of the river Derwent and Hardrada's army waiting for them. Incredibly, though, it was defended by a single man, a giant wielding a two-handed battle axe with tremendous skill. One by one Saxons charged at him, and one by one they fell at his feet, sliced in half.

Eyja was both horrified and fascinated. The man's strength and determination seemed inhuman. This was a Berserker for certain. Up until that moment she had not quite believed her father's stories. It seemed impossible that a man could possess such power. Evidently it was not, she was seeing the proof of it with her own eyes. Were all Hardrada's men like this? If they were, the Saxons didn't stand a chance.

She didn't stand a chance.

"This is ludicrous! How many more men are we going to sacrifice like this?" Moon seethed. "The more we wait here, the more time the invaders have to organize themselves. I've already seen riders leave the group on Hardrada's orders. No doubt they have gone to get reinforcements. We need to attack now, before they arrive, or we will lose the advantage we gained by taking them by surprise."

He shifted on his feet, like a bull ready to charge at its

target. Terror spiked through Eyja. Surely he wasn't considering going to face the warrior himself?

"Don't you dare go!" she barked. It seemed impossible that anyone should survive the confrontation with the man. Moon could not die before the battle had even started. If she saw him fall now, she would never have the strength to even attempt this.

"I'm not going. No one is going to get past the damn Beserker. He's too far down in his trance. We'll have to think of another way."

"There is no other way, unless someone can fly and strike him from above. Or from... underneath."

They looked at each other as she said that last word slowly, and she knew he was thinking the same thing as she was. When they were young, one of their favorite games was to try and skewer the apples from a big apple tree overhanging the river by the village. They would sit on a makeshift raft and let the current drag them underneath the laden branches, so they could try to catch a juicy fruit with a spear as they floated past it. It was hard going and they often ended up soaked but it had never failed to amuse them. And the satisfaction of actually piercing an apple as you went by was unlike anything else.

"If we can find something to act as a raft or boat, we would be able to strike him through the disjointed planks of wood," Moon said. He had reached the same conclusion as her. "It's ingenious and relatively safe. In this chaos, the man will not see you come, he's too busy fighting. And even if he does, he won't be able to reach you."

She frowned at his choice of words. *The man will not see you come.* Was he suggesting...

"What do you mean, m-me?" she stammered.

"Yes, you. You'll have to do it, Eyja," he confirmed bluntly.

Her heart skipped a beat. "You're not serious?"

"I am. You were always the best at the game, remember?

And that way you will be away from the fight, at least for a moment, without losing your honor. You will have been the one who single-handedly allowed the army to finally march on and do what it is supposed to do. We cannot keep losing so many men pointlessly like this."

As if to prove his point, at that moment, another warrior was felled, and ended up in the stream below.

She watched the corpse disappear under the surface and nodded slowly. This was the best solution for, suddenly, she could not stomach the idea of facing a swarm of snarling warriors, axe or no axe.

This was the only way she could help.

Moon saw the change in her expression and grunted. "Come. We'll try to find someone with the king's ear to suggest our idea before it's too late."

THE BRIDGE WAS IN SIGHT.

Eyja wiped the sweat from her brow while her insides dissolved in abject fear. In a moment she would have to stick her spear through a man. In other words, kill him. In cold blood. This was not an attacker running toward her in the heat of battle and she would not be raising her weapon in self-defense. She would have time to think and see it happening, she would very deliberately stick the spear she had been given into a man who didn't even know she was about to strike.

The dark deed might well haunt her for years to come, but it was too late to retreat.

She had a mission to accomplish. An important, crucial one.

King Harold had given his agreement to the plan she and Moon had presented to him. The Norseman on the bridge had to be stopped. He could not be allowed to hold the army off any longer, at the risk of seeing men die needlessly and the Norse reinforcements finally appear. He had to be killed without delay.

An empty barrel of ale had been found for her to use as a raft. It seemed she had no other choice but to go along with Moon's suggestion that she should be the one skewering their opponent, because very few of the warriors could have fit into the narrow vessel anyway. Even if she had not been volunteered, she might well have ended up in it through lack of other suitable candidates. It had been oddly satisfying to see that her being a woman—not that she would admit to it, of course—made her the best person for the crucial task. Sometimes, brute strength was simply not enough.

"You go with our prayers," the king told her before going back to his observation point.

Her mission was very clear. She was to float to the bridge, use the rope and grappling hook she'd been handed to stop right under where the Norse giant was disposing of Saxon warriors as if they were mere bugs inconveniencing him, stick her long spear through the disjointed planks and stab the man from underneath. The plan was ingenious in its simplicity, and guaranteed to work. Even if she didn't kill him outright or hurt him too seriously, the unexpected hit would be enough to allow the Saxon facing him to take advantage of the distraction to strike him down. Then, once he was dead, she was to try and reach the shore lower down the stream and join the battle as soon as possible.

Hopefully by then the army would have crossed the river and engaged in the fighting. Not that she wished it, of course, but this standoff was not working to their advantage.

"Stay out of the fight as long as you can," Moon whispered in her ear as he handed her the spear and the improvised oar she was to use to steer herself back to the shore. "Pretend the current prevented you from reaching the banks until you were a few miles downstream. There will be no shame in it, you will have done your share anyway."

Yes, it was the best solution. Except for one thing. She had to pierce a man first, and possibly kill him.

Well, what did she expect? This was war, and all in all, it was her best chance both at survival and at playing a significant role in the proceedings. In hand-to-hand combat she would be useless. Here was an unhoped for chance to do something useful.

"Ready?" Moon asked, before he and three other men lowered the barrel in which she sat into the water.

"Yes." And, for no reason that she could explain, Eyja almost reached out to kiss him.

Fortunately for her dignity, there was no way Moon and his cousin could kiss each other like lovers in front of everyone, so she was able to resist the bewildering impulse. Since when did she feel like kissing her childhood friend on the lips? Since she was about to embark on a killing mission and he was going to face mortal danger, apparently. Yes. That had to account for it. Tonight one of them, or both, could be dead. In such circumstances, she might well have wanted to kiss anyone dear to her, just to make her feel better.

"Take care of yourself, Moon, please," she murmured.

His eyes sent sparks. "You too, Imp. I'll see you after the battle."

The battle. How soon it might happen now all hinged on her.

The bridge was drawing near. It was now or never, soon she would be swept away by the current and it would be too late. There would be no second chance, she would never be able to paddle her way back upstream for another try.

With great care, Eyja swung the rope and threw her grappling hook. It caught on one of the wooden posts, slowing her down. So far so good. Using all her strength, she pulled to position herself where she needed to be, in the middle of the bridge, and straight underneath the Norse warrior. She could hear the grunts of the two fighters above her. Something fell on her forehead. When she realized it was blood, shock almost caused her to let go of the rope. No, she had managed to position herself, she could not let go now, she could not falter! For more safety, she wrapped the rope around her middle.

There.

Even if she let go in a moment of panic, she wouldn't ruin her chances.

Holding on with her left hand, she took the spear in her right and thrust upward. Nothing. She lowered the weapon and did it again, harder, higher. This time it made contact. A scream split the air and a heartbeat later she heard a shout of triumph, followed by the sound of dozens of warriors running onto the bridge to finish off the formidable enemy. Moments later the corpse of the mighty warrior she had felled was thrown over into the river in front of her eyes. Though rationally she knew this time it was water, not blood, splashing her, Eyja could not help a scream of horror.

For a long moment she stayed there, trembling. Then slowly she reopened her eyes and breathed in deeply. Her part was over.

She let go of the rope and allowed the current to sweep her away.

CHAPTER FIVE

In the end, Eyja did not have to pretend to struggle to make it back to the shore.

Once she passed the bridge the current picked up, sweeping her away from the mayhem at great speed, and it took all her dwindling strength and more time than she had expected to steer the barrel toward the riverbank. Eventually, she made it. Panting hard with exhaustion, she allowed herself a moment of respite on the grassy shore before dragging herself up and starting the long walk back to the site of the battle. It took a while, because she was wet and shaking in the aftermath of her shock, and she had a cumbersome spear in her hand. Moon, who would have to go into the melee with the others from the start, had kept both axes. While she walked, she tried to find comfort in the fact that he was as armed as he could be. Who could survive an attack by a man like him wielding two blades? Who would even dare approach him? Only madmen.

No, he had to survive. She could not think of the alternative.

By the time Eyja reached the battlefield, more exhausted than she had ever been in her entire life, the fighting was almost over. The field was littered with corpses, the few Norsemen still standing had been herded into a corner and the king was discussing what was to be done with them. Everything and everyone was tainted with blood. It was a nightmarish vision.

She understood from what bits of conversation she overheard that both Hardrada and the king's brother had been killed, but the news failed to raise any reaction out of her. There was only one thing on her mind.

Or rather, some*one*.

Moon. She had to find him before she went mad.

She searched the field for the only man she wanted to see, not knowing whether to look on the ground amongst the dead or ahead, amongst the exhausted warriors stumbling around covered in blood and dirt.

The more devastation she saw, the more unlikely it seemed that Moon could have survived such a massacre. How would she bear it if he had died and she toppled over his mutilated corpse? Would she even recognize him if he'd been butchered? A thought crossed her mind. Even if his face had been hacked at out of all recognition, at least she would know him by the moon mark on his wrist.

She forced herself to put the grim thought from her mind. She would not despair until she knew for sure that he was dead. Her heart stopped for a moment when she spotted braided, long blond hair streaked with blood on a man lying face down in the mud. Fighting back nausea, she turned him around. Seeing a dead man's face was the last thing she wanted to do but it was the only way she could ascertain his identity. To her relief, the warrior she stared at was not the one she had dreaded to recognize.

And then she saw him.

Towering over the others, his glorious blond hair shining like a beacon, he was standing some distance away, with his back to her, an axe in each hand. Solid. Alive. She ran, then stopped when he turned to face her, as if warned by an inaudible voice that she was headed his way.

"By the gods," she thought she heard him say.

She wanted to throw herself into his arms but at the last moment remembered who she was supposed to be. A man. Men did not do that. They nodded, or slapped one another on the shoulder at the most. She stopped inches away from him, not wanting to do that when she felt so emotional. It would be ridiculous. They looked at each other for a few heartbeats then, heedless of who might see them, Moon wrapped an arm around her neck to bring her close.

Eyja could not have drawn away if her life depended on it. The embrace, rough and masculine as it was, was perhaps more intimate than cousins would share, but would probably not be enough to raise suspicion amidst men who were busy wading through the dead. If Moon thought it plausible for him to act in that manner, she would not question it. It felt too good to be in his arms after fearing he had died. His voice reached her, rougher than usual.

"You did it, Imp. I knew we could trust you."

"You made it," she almost sobbed against his shoulder. "I knew you would."

For a moment they basked in each other's warmth and the relief of knowing they were unscathed, then they drew away, looking rather self-conscious. A manly embrace in the wake of battle was one thing, a prolonged cuddle quite another. Eyja raked her gaze over him, while he did the same with her. It was only then she saw the blood on his tunic, the grime on his face, the sweat on his brow—and the cut on his thigh.

"But, you're injured!"

"Yes," he said tersely, as if it didn't matter. "Like everyone else. But 'tis nothing. We won. Both Tostig and Hardrada are dead. The Norsemen were annihilated. The only thing left for them now is to run back home with their tails between their legs. We've made it."

Just then, as if to confirm his words, someone slapped Moon on the shoulder. "A great victory, hey, Norseman! I'm glad to see that no one cut you in half."

Farmon, obviously. Eyja stifled a scream when she saw the wound splitting his cheek in half. It was horrific and would be painful. He paid it no more mind that she would to a scratch, however.

Moon took a step away from her before answering. "More than one man tried. But I hit them first."

"I bet you did. Well, I don't mind admitting I had my doubts about you and your cousin. They have now been put to rest. You certainly did your share in disposing of the savages." He laughed as if he'd said something very witty. No one laughed with him. "Let's go and wash the grime away. We finally have time to relax and see to our needs. I should think we've earned it, after so many days with barely enough time to piss."

Eyja and Moon exchanged a glance. Though she was desperate to rid herself of the blood, dust and sweat crusting her body, she obviously could not undress in front of the men. But how to refuse to join them without raising suspicion? A good number of Saxons had already stripped down to plunge them-selves into the cool river below.

"You go. Eirik and I will wash tonight in the moonlight, like all Norsemen do," Moon said matter-of-factly.

"You wash at night?" Farmon sounded incredulous, as well he might.

"Of course. The moon is sacred for us people, we wouldn't dare to risk Máni's wrath by washing at any other time than when he's pulling his chariot. We wouldn't want the wolf Hati Hrodvitnisson to catch him up and devour him because of a mistake we made, now would we? My family is especially devoted to Máni. Why do you think my people call me Moon when you know my name is Halfdan? No, battle or not, we'll honor our traditions and wait."

The men stared at the avalanche of foreign names and ideas. Eyja worked hard not to stare as well. Where had all that come from? Since when did her people wash at night? Would Farmon not think them mad? Perhaps. But at least there was no more talk of them joining the people bathing.

Once the Saxons had gone away, grumbling to themselves that Norsemen were decidedly too odd to be believed, she turned to Moon, brow arched.

"Well, did you have a better idea?" he asked before she could even open her mouth.

"No." It had been genius on his part. Indeed they'd had to make up a reason why she could not strip in front of them without raising the men's suspicions and he'd come up with the perfect one.

"The Saxons already see us as savages, with customs and habits they don't understand. I could have claimed that we like to bathe in salted goat milk and whip ourselves with ropes afterward, they would have believed it. Why not make the most of it?"

Why not indeed?

"Thank you. I had no idea how to refuse the offer. But you don't mind waiting to get cleaned up?" She could not join the men, but he didn't have the same problem. It was a hot day, and he would no doubt be itching to plunge his body in the cool water.

"No. After waiting five days for it, I think I can wait another moment. Night will fall soon enough. And first, I'd like to eat and drink. I'm ravenous and we finally have time to enjoy some peace and quiet."

Eyja sighed and looked at the sky above them. "Yes. We do."

"WHAT ARE YOU DOING?"

Moon stared at Eyja, who stared back at him as if he'd gone mad for asking the question. "I'm getting undressed. Isn't that what people do before they bathe? Or do you think that, as eccentric Norsemen, we should only be naked when we eat cheese or feed the chickens?"

He cleared his throat, ignoring her teasing. Well, yes, getting undressed to have a wash was the normal thing to do, but...

Suddenly, being naked seemed the last thing she should do in his presence.

"I don't think it's a good idea." He barely managed to get the words out. There seemed to be an egg-sized lump in his throat—and an unwelcome bulge in his braies. No, not again! It was like the other night, only this time it was even more inexplicable. They weren't touching, and he hadn't seen as much as her bare feet. What was happening to him? It had to be the aftermath of the battle that affected him, he decided. Hadn't he heard that people who narrowly escaped death experienced a surge of desire, the need to express their joy and relief at being alive?

Yes, that was probably what it was.

"Come. Don't tell me you've gone all shy? How many times have we bathed in front of each other?" She let out a giggle and reached for her other boot.

"Dozens of times, but we were children."

"So?" She didn't seem to see his point. But he saw it only too well. Now he was a grown man, and in his grown man's brain, seeing a woman naked, no matter how legitimate the reason, was no innocent act. That Eyja was a friend he'd known all his life did not change facts. She was a woman, and in the last few days he had become acutely, painfully aware of the fact. After the other night, when he'd been aroused to feel her atop him, he was not ready to see her naked. He was not at all sure he would handle it well.

He shrugged, as if he didn't really mind one way or another, but simply had to be sensible.

"We'll take turns to bathe. That way I can keep watch in case one of the men chooses this moment to have a wash as well," he said with decision. "It wouldn't do for them to see your body, as they would understand what you are, and that's what we've been trying to avoid all along. Stay under water while you wash, and keep your shirt on for as long as possible."

He fully expected her to argue but, to his relief, she nodded. He turned around, ostensibly to keep an eye out for intruders. In reality, he was making sure he didn't get even the slightest glimpse of her smooth, white flesh gilded by the moonlight and wet from the river water.

But not seeing her did not stop his imagination from running amok.

Although he had always chosen his lovers for their voluptuous figures, he had to admit that there was a certain grace about Eyja's lithe form. He could not deny being curious. How would she look, with her small, pert breasts and slender thighs? How would she feel under his palms? All taut and muscular probably, nothing like a woman who spent her days sewing and cooking inside the hut. His fingers were itching to find out. And with her fiery nature and impressive strength, he guessed she would be a most adventurous and vigorous bed partner, one who would not shy away from the boldest caresses and be able to ride him for long moments without tiring.

Yes... perhaps he'd had it all wrong. Perhaps a petite, impetuous woman was the lover he needed, not a soft, pampered one.

When he heard the splash of water announcing she had plunged into the river, he willed himself not to look over his shoulder but he heard her sigh of relief as she washed away the grime of the past few days. He couldn't wait to do the same.

"It's your turn," she called after a moment. Moon couldn't have said how long she'd been in the water. All he knew was that his body was on fire. A plunge in the icy river was just what he needed right now. "Hurry. You wouldn't want Hati Hrodvit-nisson to devour you, now, would you?"

"You really are an imp, you know that?" he muttered between his teeth.

"I would be hard pressed not to, as you keep calling me that."

He ignored the retort. Of course she knew she was an imp.

"Are you dressed?" he asked instead. She'd said it was his turn, which didn't necessarily mean that she had put her clothes back on. For all he knew she was stark naked and stretching, oblivious to the temptation she represented for a hot-blooded male.

"Yes. It's safe for you to turn around," she answered, sounding mightily amused. "You won't be turned into stone upon seeing me."

Well, he was not so sure about that, Part of him already *had* turned to stone.

"Really, you're impossible, you—"

Moon turned around and stopped mid-sentence because, though she was not naked, Eyja was not quite dressed either. All he could do was stare at the pure white column of her throat, revealed by the gaping collar of Ari's oversized shirt. It was so big on her that he could see the top of two round breasts which appeared to be just as pert as he'd thought. Even worse, the cold of the water had made her nipples hard as pebbles and they were pointing straight at him, as if to challenge him to take a bite. He lowered his gaze before he surrendered to the urge to do just that. A mistake. The hem of the shirt only reached mid-thigh, drawing attention to the two slender legs he tried very hard not to imagine wrapped around his waist while he plunged inside her.

Damn and blast, she was delectable, it wasn't safe to look *anywhere*, not even her feet! He knew because he'd already noticed that they were as perfect and delicate as any he had ever seen.

"I wish I had other clothes to put back on now that I am clean," Eyja said, oblivious to the workings of his overheated mind. "Everything is filthy but I cannot wash them as I have nothing else to wear and cannot sleep in wet clothes."

She sighed and bent down to pick up her braies. As she lifted one leg to put them on, she let out a small groan. All lewd thoughts instantly vanished from Moon's mind and he planted himself in front of her, steadying her with his hands at the shoulders. What was he doing, gaping at her instead of enquiring after her health?

"What's the matter? Are you injured?" She hadn't seemed to be, but he could not be certain. Under the grime, she could have hidden all manners of cuts and bruises. He should have asked before, but when he'd seen her standing, alive and whole on that battlefield, he'd forgotten everything.

She shook her head. "No, I'm just a bit sore everywhere, that's all. I fear that now it's all over, my body will make me pay for what I put it through these last few days."

Yes, he could well imagine. His might as well.

"Go and get some sleep now. It's already late." To keep up the pretense they weren't avoiding the others, they'd had to wait until the moon was high in the sky to go and have a wash, thereby forgoing some precious resting time. "I won't be long."

Eyja started to walk back to the place they had selected for the night then realized she would rather wait for Moon. She felt safer amidst the men when he was around, all strong and dependable. He must be as exhausted as she was, and eager to get some sleep, so he would not be long.

A little delay couldn't hurt.

She retraced her steps and skidded to a halt when his naked form appeared through the branches. He was standing knee high in the water, looking into the distance, still as a statue. For a brief moment, she considered averting her eyes. Then, as if to ensure her gaze remained fixed on him, he bent down to gather water into his cupped hands and let it trickle down over his head. In that instant, King Hardrada himself could have come back from the dead to charge at her, she would not have found the will to look away from Moon. It was a vision of pure decadence, one that did odd things to her insides. Wet, his hair was darker and even longer than usual, fanning over his shoulder blades in a sheet of silk. He was perfection, except for one thing. The smooth skin was mottled by cuts and bruises scattered all over his body, proof that the battle had been hard fought. But it did not distract from his beauty in any way, if anything, it even enhanced it, since it proved his courage and strength.

Would she ever be able to get that image of masculine beauty out of her mind? Eyja snorted when she realized that she would not even try. Why would she do such a foolish thing? It could be something she would cherish until her dying day.

The noise she made must have alerted him to her presence because he turned, and saw her.

Oh. My.

The back had been perfect, the front was... spectacular. The God of the Moon Máni himself could not be more chiseled, more perfect than this. Moon had been right. Everything was different now. They were not children anymore. His body was definitely not that of a child anymore. The muscular shoulders, the broad chest, the blond hairs following the contours of his taunt stomach, the...

All the air left her lungs when her gaze landed on the member gracing the apex of his thighs.

No, he was most definitely not the boy she had known before, but all man. Had he not been her brother's friend she might well have stepped forward and asked if she could touch him. As he *was* Torsten's best friend, and they had grown up together, she refrained from throwing herself into his arms and begging him to let her stroke him.

"I told you to go," he said, his voice hoarse. She noticed that he made no move to cover his nudity, for which she was grateful. Such beauty should never be hidden.

"I stayed." Obviously. Why has she said that? He could see that for himself.

"Do you ever do what you're supposed to do, Imp?"

"I don't know."

Another stupid answer. But all her thoughts had scattered at the sight of his glorious body. Her blood was singing in her veins and her mind had definitely ground to a halt. And perhaps she was not the only one affected by the moment. Because since he'd seen her, Moon's attitude had started to change. His breathing had gone faster, the member she had admired earlier was no longer lying limply against his thigh, and it was getting even thicker, harder. She knew what it meant.

Heat burnt her cheeks

"Are you—"

He disappeared under the water before she could finish the sentence. When his head broke through the surface again, Eyja still had not taken a breath, as if she'd been the one submerged in the stream.

"Go," Moon barked, remaining hidden from the neck down. "You need to sleep."

"I... I don't want to go back to the camp without you. It doesn't feel safe."

This was not a lie or an excuse to stay by the river and ogle him. Cleaned up, in front of a man who felt desire for her, Eyja had never felt more like a woman, more vulnerable. It seemed to her that all the men would see through her disguise in that moment, something she could not afford, now even less than before, because now they had time to make the most of the discovery.

Being a woman amongst warriors drunk on their victory was no place to be.

Moon muttered something under his breath. It was probably for the best she couldn't catch what it was because she had no doubt he was cursing her for disobeying his orders.

"Turn around then," he ordered sharply. He seemed as aggravated as the night she had tried to tickle him. "And make sure you do what you're supposed to do for once."

She turned her back without a word of protest but in truth, she wasn't sure she could have handled watching him emerge, wet and glistening, from the water. Then, friend or no friend, she *would* have thrown herself at him.

There were a few splashing sounds, then silence, followed by the rustle of clothes. Eventually, Moon joined her. She didn't look at him, or he at her. They simply stood side by side a moment, breathing hard.

"Come then, let's go sleep."

CHAPTER SIX

For a blissful couple of days the army of bedraggled men took the rest they deserved. They finally had time to sleep, eat, and drink as much as they needed. They also tended to the numerous wounds they had suffered. Moon had been right. As far as Eyja could tell, she was the only one who did not bear any cuts. But no one dared mock her for it. As soon as someone started to question her courage, Moon told them about the felling of the Norse giant, which had all been down to her. They all went silent then, knowing how much they owed her.

To her relief, the cut to Moon's thigh was healing well. He'd been right about that too. All in all, he'd been lucky. He'd not even required any stitching

They were starting to wonder what they would do next when they received disastrous news.

All the way down south, a new menace was brewing. A fleet of Normans, led by the Duke of Normandy, had landed on the coast. The king, who had been expecting them for weeks, hastily assembled his men again and announced they would march at dawn. Eyja looked at Moon in consternation. She could not face another grueling march and another battle to the death. This was not why she had left her village. Because of her dual heritage she had felt the need to repel the Norse invaders, but she felt no such urge with Normans, much less now that she had seen the reality of war.

"I don't want to go," she murmured, not caring if he thought her a coward. However brave she was, she was not suited to the role of a warrior.

The words had barely passed her lips than Farmon came to them, flanked as per usual by his pack of men. Half of them were limping, the other half sported horrific wounds on their faces but they had all survived the attack. This didn't surprise her. They seemed like a fierce, indomitable lot and she wondered, not for the first time, why they followed Farmon as if they owed their allegiance to him. Perhaps they did, for some reason or other, and they had not truly chosen to be here. It was not impossible.

The man had tyrant written all over his face.

"Listen," the Saxon said. "I'm not going back south to fight the Normans. It was one thing facing savages from the north, quite another fighting civilized people following a man who has a real claim to the throne."

Eyja usually did as Moon had ordered her on the first day, and spoke as little as possible when in the presence of Saxons. She therefore ignored the slur against her own people, but nevertheless it grated to be called a savage, when other invaders were called civilized.

"Aye, I heard that Duke William of Normandy had been promised the throne by the late king," Moon agreed, surprising her. She'd had no idea he kept himself abreast of such developments. Then again, they had never discussed politics together at the village. "He was then betrayed by Harold Godwinson, who had himself crowned in haste at the death of King Edward."

Well, if that were true, she could hardly blame the Norman for wanting to secure what was rightfully his. Eyja welcomed the news, which only comforted her in her decision to leave the army now. This quarrel had nothing to do with her. She had only meant to appease her conscience by making sure she could hold her head high when Saxons accused her of being one of the invaders.

"This is not our fight," Farmon agreed, gesturing at his men. For once, they were in full agreement. "We are going back home. I think you feel the same, so I am here to offer that we travel back south together. The larger our group is, the safer it will be for all of us."

Moon looked at her, as if to ask her opinion. She nodded. He already knew that she had only meant to go fight the Norse menace so he would not be surprised by her decision.

"We do feel the same." He spoke for both of them, for which she was grateful. "We had our reasons to stop the Norsemen, as I said, but the Normans are quite different. It has nothing to do with the fact that they are supposedly more civilized than Hardrada's men, though. It is only that we believe they have a valid claim and I will not be dragged into men's petty squabbles."

Farmon gave a smile. He had not missed the remonstrance and seemed to like Moon's pluck.

"It is agreed then. I don't think they will notice our absence or bother coming after us. We might not even be the only ones leaving but they won't have the time or the men to try and get us back We'll leave together tonight."

THE WALK back to the village bore little resemblance to the march of the army to York. There was no sense of urgency, time enough to eat and sleep in the evenings, and talk during the day.

For all that, it was not what Moon would have called pleasant. It was safer for them to travel in a group, so he had no choice but to endure it, but really, Farmon and his friends were a crass, unruly lot, something he had already suspected but was now proven in spectacular fashion. He'd lost count of the number of times he'd had to grit his teeth instead of asking them to stop their bawdy jests. Though he could see she was fuming on the inside at the way they talked about people, and women in particular, Eyja bore it all like a... well, like a man. Doing anything else would have drawn attention to her, but her calm took him by surprise. The imp was not exactly renowned for her patience so the way she kept a tight leash on her temper impressed him. Apparently, she had more control over her impulses than he'd suspected.

On the third morning, however, she finally snapped.

They were breaking their fasts before setting off and Farmon was complaining about the length of time he'd had to go without female company, a recurring theme in the men's discussions, as was to be expected. They had been doing nothing but march and fight for over a week now.

"We should find women to see to our needs in the next town we reach," he declared, ripping a piece of rabbit flesh with as much finesse as a starving dog. "After what we did, you'll agree that we've earned a little reward. I would like nothing more than to lie back and watch a woman suck my cock. She can do all the work, I've done my share against the savages, I should think."

"Aye, so would I. A woman... or three." The men laughed and agreed, adding their own lewd propositions to the discussion, which quickly became a veritable list of debauched acts.

Moon stole a glance at Eyja, suspecting she would have

gone bright red. She probably had no idea men and women could do all this together.

"What about you, young Eirik?" Farmon asked, turning to her. "Fancy a good poke? Or are you still a virgin? Tell you what, if you don't know how it's done, you can watch me plough one of the whores. That should get you in the mood for some action."

"Why would I want to do that?" she replied in a calm voice that did nothing to minimize the spark in her eyes. Moon tensed up. He knew that look all too well. She was about to explode. "Watching a pig roll in mud will be as likely to get me aroused as watching you rut. And I doubt you know what you're doing if you prefer to let the women do all the work. So I think I'll figure out what to do on my own, thank you."

Whistles welcomed this sally. The men had liked the spirited answer. Farmon, however, had not. He threw the rabbit bone into the fire and bared his teeth in a grimace. "You impudent little—"

Moon stood up before the Saxon could launch himself at Eyja and took her by the arm.

"Come with me," he instructed tersely. "Now."

"Why?" she asked in Norse, ignoring the fact that he had pointedly spoken in a language the men would understand.

He glared at her. He'd wanted to make it look as if he was about to explain to his disrespectful little cousin that he owed his elders some respect. That way she might be allowed to get out of this unscathed, because he feared that in the absence of whores to offer him relief, Farmon would decide that pounding a frail Norseman to the ground was another, efficient way to alleviate his frustration.

"We are going to have a little discussion, you and I."

Eyja didn't see how she could refuse. Moon was furious. She knew she had gone too far so she followed without comment while the Saxons kept on laughing. No doubt the idiots thought he was about to remonstrate with her—him—for mocking their self-appointed leader's ability to pleasure women.

"What did you want to talk about?" she asked as meekly as she could, which was probably not very. At least Moon did not appear impressed by her efforts at appeasement. Anger was radiating through his every pore.

"What the *hell* were you thinking, provoking the fool thus? He's a crude, dangerous bastard."

Though it was the last thing she should do, Eyja couldn't help it. She smiled. Moon really was his father's son when he wanted to be. Sigurd had a foul mouth and she'd had ample opportunity over the last week to see that the son had inherited it. Thus far in the village he'd seemed able to control his tongue in her presence. Now, possibly because she was posing as a man, he did not even try to stop himself. She liked it. It showed he was not afraid to be himself in front of her and trusted her to know he was no dumb brute for all that.

Well, she would return the favor and not try to spare him from her thoughts. She was not sorry she had put the awful man in his place.

"I could not bear his comments a moment longer. Did you not hear what he said just now? What he's been saying for days? How he sees women? How he mocked me for being a virgin and boasted about his supposed—"

"Yes, I did hear all that, thank you." He made a cutting gesture. "But you're not really my cousin, but a woman, in case you'd forgotten, and the last thing you should do is—"

"Stop using that as an excuse when we both know you don't see me as a woman!"

"I don't?"

He looked as bewildered as if she had just admitted to being a winged horse. But Eyja was not so easily silenced because she knew she was right. Moon had never seen her as a woman and they both knew it.

It had never been a problem, but suddenly, and without knowing quite why, she was incensed that he only allowed himself to see her as Eirik, a young lad he could go to war with, and not Eyja, a woman he could feel desire for. Twice now, the evening she had tickled him and the night they had bathed in the river, she had seen the proof that he could be aroused in her presence but twice she'd been forced to accept that it bothered him, as if it were unnatural that he should find *her* desirable. He was angry at his body's reaction because it didn't match what he thought of her.

"Of course, you don't. Admit it. Our whole lives you've seen me as my parents' fourth son, to be treated the way you treated my other brothers. If you saw me as a girl, you wouldn't have thrown me in the lake that day I went swimming with you and Steinar, would you? You wouldn't have sparred with me in the mud like you did with Torsten and you most certainly would have waited until I was out of hearing range before you told Sven all about the first girl you'd bedded." Sobs started to swell inside her chest. "I was always one of the lads for you. Not a girl then, and not a woman now."

And today, it hurt.

She pushed at his chest in her anguish. He was so unprepared for it, and she so fueled by disillusion that she actually managed to topple him over. They tumbled down to the floor together when they both lost their balance, Moon ending up on top of her. The provocative position and the fact that he barely seemed to notice it, did nothing to calm her frustration. Couldn't he see that it was not normal for a man to be between a woman's legs and not even think of taking advantage of the fact? Wasn't he supposed to want to make the most of the opportunity?

"See, you don't see me as a woman, you never have! A companion, a sister at best, a nuisance at worst, but not a woman." Never someone he could take to bed. She let out the sob that had been building in her throat. Why did it matter so much how he saw her all of a sudden? She had no idea, but it did.

"I do see you as a woman, how could I not?" Moon growled. "I've known you all my life, I'm not fooled by your disguise. I know who you are."

Yes, he knew but he didn't care, which was even worse. Would he be talking calmly while she was under him if he saw her as someone he could seduce? Would he ignore the way their two bodies were pressed against each other? No. He'd known her all his life. And that was the problem. She was part of the landscape, nothing more.

She'd known Björn's son Rorik all her life as well, and yet he had not hesitated in kissing her when she'd asked him to. And Thorfinn had done much more than that, *he* had definitely treated her as a woman, taking her hand to place it on his throbbing member, demanding that she pleasured him. Moon would never even think of stealing as much a kiss, never mind take liberties with her.

"Tell me this then. What would you do if you found yourself on top of a woman thus? Wouldn't you want more? Wouldn't you think of fucking her?"

He stilled. "By the gods, Eyja, where have you learned such words? And what do you know about f— about that anyway?"

She stared at him, incredulous. For three days it was all she'd heard Farmon and his friends talk about. Did he really think she would not have picked up on the words they used? Besides, and though she did not want to talk about it now, thanks to Thorfinn, she was not as inexperienced as he seemed to think.

"I am not quite the innocent you take me for. I have been kissed, you know," she replied, piqued in her self-esteem. Some men desired her, even if he didn't. "And I have ears."

"You certainly do. We wouldn't be here if you had not overheard my conversation with Torsten about joining the army, now would we?"

Irritation washed over her. Here he was again, talking to her as he would to a childhood companion. She didn't want to discuss the reasons for her presence here, not while they were talking about the normal way for a man and a woman to behave when they found themselves one on top of the other.

"Never mind that! I was asking you a question. Answer me. If you saw me as a woman, wouldn't you be trying to f—"

"No, I wouldn't!" he exploded before she could repeat the crude word. "Because I know you're untouched."

This did nothing to placate her. Once again that was not what she was talking about. Virgins could still be kissed and desired. They could still be touched and caressed, they could touch and caress in return. He was only holding on to miserable excuses.

"So what if I am? Are you telling me you have a conscience? Or are you not enough of a man to—"

"Enough!"

From the roar with which the word was uttered, Eyja knew that she had pushed Moon over the edge. There would be no coming back from this. At last! Excitement filled her. What would he do now? There was such power, such heat radiating from his body that hers seemed to catch fire.

"I'll show you what I do to infuriating minxes who provoke me!" he muttered between his teeth, raising himself above her so as to slip a hand between their two bodies.

Without another word he reached down to the waistband of her hose and yanked them down roughly. She yelped, never having seen this fiery, savage side of him before. She was suddenly reminded that his father had been called 'Beast' in his youth. Only a moment ago she'd thought Moon was his true son because he liked to swear. She'd had no idea how deep the resemblance ran. In that moment he did put her in mind of a beast.

A beast who was about to devour her.

Excitement became trepidation. Had she gone too far? They were not so far away from the group of Saxons who were getting ready to depart. Was it really wise to get intimate now, here?

"Wait, Moon..."

But he didn't seem to hear her, which did not surprise her. She might not have had enough air in her lungs to say the words out loud. Or perhaps she had only thought them, she didn't know. With his hands on her bare skin, her mind was all in disarray.

"Well, this I haven't done before, that's for sure," he grumbled while he tugged at her braies. No, she imagined he hadn't undressed many men in his days. His tastes didn't run that way. "Where are skirts when you need them?"

Was he really going to do this? Get her naked and take her, like the woman she was? Finally, he freed one of her legs from the hose and stared at the curls he had just revealed with fierce intent. She thought she heard him groan but she could barely hear anything over the beating in her chest.

"Moon..." she started again, not sure what to say, because she was unsure she was ready to take such a momentous step as to be fully possessed by a man right here, right now.

"Spread your legs," he ordered.

Everything went liquid inside Eyja. She should never have provoked him so. He looked half demented with desire. Oh, what had she done? Of course she knew he was man enough for anything she could think of and more!

He was the image of the formidable lover, tall and strong. Confident.

"Spread your legs for me," he repeated when she remained frozen in uncertainty.

To make sure she obeyed this time, he placed both hands on her thighs. He did not force her to open them, but he made sure she did not close them again when she finally allowed her knees to fall to the sides. His nostrils flared and his eyes caught fire when he saw her exposed to him. Eyja whimpered. The position was so lewd, she was so confused and aroused, she wasn't sure how long she would bear the scrutiny. This was beyond intimate.

"What are you going to do?" she croaked.

"Oh now you're wondering? After all your talk of fucking, after all the teasing, *now* you're afraid of what I might do?"

"I'm not afraid."

Not of him, never that. She knew him too well to know he would never hurt her. But she could not deny being out of her depth. As a virgin with very little experience of men, she wasn't sure what to expect. All she knew was that he was still fully dressed. Her heart tripped in her chest. Inexperienced as she was, she knew that he at least needed to bare his shaft to take her. So perhaps that was not what he had in mind? Perhaps he would simply use his fingers to pleasure her, like Thorfinn had done? She instantly dissolved in anticipation, knowing it would feel even better with him.

"I'm not afraid," she repeated, her voice husky with need.

"Good. You need not be afraid." He lowered himself and rested his weight on his elbows. "I'm not going to hurt you or even take you, only show you what I do to virgins."

She'd been right then, he was going to plunge his fingers inside her.

He did not.

His hands remained firmly on her thighs, keeping them wide open, and his tongue darted out instead. Eyja's fevered brain struggled to make sense of what she was seeing. Was he about to... lick her? His tongue, was that what he meant to use to pleasure her? It could not be. Her body, not so easily shocked, manifested its approval in every way it could. Before she could stop herself, she arched her back in search for more. Moon bent his head. A heartbeat later, she felt his tongue, hot and velvety, slide along the part of herself that proved without doubt she was the woman she had claimed to be.

Eyja cried out. "Are you mad?" Fingers were one thing, but *this*? She had not expected this! Even Farmon and his friends, with all their crude talk, had never alluded to such scandalous dealings. If you listened to them, only women used their mouths and tongues to pleasure their lovers, not the other way around.

"No, I'm not mad," was Moon's answer. "But I promise to send you mad with need. And to make you explode in pleasure."

She was now trembling. "But... why?"

Shut up! Her mind instantly rebelled. *Who cares why he wants to do this, as long as he does!*

"It will be your punishment for saying I didn't see you as a woman, for thinking I was not man enough to take you. After that, you will never be able to doubt either of those things again. Now hush, and let me proceed."

Moon had no idea what had gotten hold of him.

He'd meant to put an end to Eyja's teasing, to silence the wretched woman and show her it was a dangerous thing to play with a man's pride and stoke his desire when he was already aroused. But now...

Now he was overcome with lust.

Eyja was right. All his life he'd seen her as a friend, at the best of times, a nuisance at worst. The younger sister who'd constantly been in the way when he wanted to play with her brothers, a companion he'd had no choice but to accept in the band, a reckless imp who'd launched herself headlong into an enterprise that was not her own.

Over the last week she'd caused him endless worry, forced him to sleep with one eye open when he needed rest, turned his life into a living hell with the bewildering desire she provoked inside him. He'd twisted his mind into knots doing what was needed to provide her with the protection she needed, thought of nothing else than her. Her, with her disturbing cropped hair, and ridiculous men's clothes, her with her brazenness and utter inability to hold her tongue when it was needed. All those things should have ensured he could remain detached in his dealings with her.

It had not. What in another would have been seen as faults seemed like qualities in her. Because he could not think of anyone else combining these with courage and honesty and mischief. There was no one quite like her. For days he had done his best to consider her no different from the men around them, marching toward battle—and failed.

And now...

Now it was all over, they were headed back home and there was time to think. Now she had seen him bathe and not averted her eyes, he had felt her writhe atop him, he had gone hard imagining her naked body.

Now everything was changed.

There was nothing ridiculous about her. She wasn't an imp playing at being a man anymore, or a nuisance, or someone who'd been forced on him. Now she was in his arms and she was all woman, feminine and sweet-smelling. Her body, half bared to him, was beautiful. Her legs, finally free of those awful braies, were long, slender and downy soft. Her sex, so close to his waiting mouth, was weeping for him. Her scent was intoxicating. He already knew she would taste like melted butter and honey, his favorite treat, and he couldn't wait to get his fill of her. He knew he could not take her and would have to see to his release on his own afterward, but he needed this indulgence.

Licking her was sure to bring him to the brink of orgasm. Once she'd been satisfied, he would take himself in hand and finish it off. It was the only option he had, because he could not take her maidenhead. That was not what this was about.

Eyja moaned and Moon stopped thinking. To hell with Farmon and his men, to hell with what he should do, to hell with the consequences. He needed this.

"Hush," he repeated as he dipped his head to the sweet temptation awaiting him. "Now let me feast. If you need to scream, scream into your hand."

CHAPTER SEVEN

She did need to scream. Badly. Eyja bit her bottom lip so hard to stop herself from uttering a sound, she tasted blood. She needed to scream so much she feared she would burst with the effort needed to contain it.

Using his lips, his tongue, his teeth, Moon was devouring her.

No, not devour, she amended with the last ounce of clarity she possessed. That was too negative a word. What he was doing was...

She had no idea what it was. Extraordinary. Life changing? Nothing like what she had felt under Thorfinn's caresses, that was for sure.

"I can't... Oh, please..." she panted, searching the ground around her for something to hold on to. She only encountered grass. Far from heeding her protests, Moon grunted and lifted her left leg onto his shoulder as if to give him better access. A finger circled her intimate opening then pushed inside slowly. The feeling was so incredible she let out a mewl. And then another, and another. His tongue never ceased lapping at her all through the onslaught.

Oh, this was going to kill her.

But she would die a happy woman.

Trembling, she dug her fingers into his hair, anchoring him in place, forcing him to come closer. She would die if he stopped now, if he retreated even one fraction of an inch. An almost unbearable heat had started to bloom inside her chest. She wanted to rip at her shirt, feel the cool air on her skin. And then...

And then she imploded in a burst of light.

A scream escaped her throat but it made no noise. There was no air left in her lungs, no strength in her limbs, nothing left of her but the part pulsating against Moon's hot mouth. Merciful gods, his *mouth*. His mouth had been on her, she had opened her legs for his kisses, had pressed herself against his face, had forced him to lick her harder and to plunge his finger deeper inside.

After sharing such intimacy, she would never be able to look at him again without blushing and remembering the feel of his lips on her. And he would never be able to look at her without tasting her on his tongue. How would they ever recover from there? Whatever they had been to each other, they could never be again. Could they find another way?

She wasn't sure.

In any case, she could not think right now, she could only lie, eyes closed, body empty and limp, mind blank.

She felt him straighten back up, withdraw his finger from her, then heard the rustle of fabric as he tugged at his clothes. Dimly, Eyja wondered if he was now going to take her, or ask her to pleasure him in turn, like Thorfinn had done. In all probability he was hard and ready for his own release. But he didn't ask anything, didn't even touch or speak to her. Kneeling next to her prone form, he saw to his needs himself. It did not take long. There was a series of grunts and groans and then silence.

After a long moment, just as Eyja thought she would fall asleep there on the forest floor, she felt Moon crawl up to her and put his mouth at her ear.

"Don't provoke me like this again, Imp. I am perfectly able to fuck women and I can't promise that the next time I won't do just that."

"So... Halfdan's little 'cousin' is in fact a woman. Well. I should have guessed."

Eyja froze in the act of fastening her braies when the nasal voice she had come to hate reached her ear.

Farmon.

Slowly, hoping to be mistaken even though she knew she could not be, she turned to face him.

"Not only a woman but one who enjoys getting fucked," he carried on, walking toward her with deliberate intent. "I've never seen anyone rub herself so frantically against a man's face. *Quite* an arousing sight."

At first she was horrified by the crude description. Had she really done that? Rubbed herself shamelessly against Moon's face? And then the full meaning of his words hit her, eclipsing everything else. Farmon had watched her and Moon in their most intimate moment and gotten aroused by it. Not only that but he'd then waited for Moon to walk away to make his presence known. This could only mean one thing.

Now that he knew her real identity, he meant to make the most of it, and take her himself.

She scrambled back to her feet and looked around in case Moon had decided to come back for her. Should she call him? He could not be too far away. Why oh why had she not tried to stop him when he'd gone back to the camp? Mortified or not by what they had done, she shouldn't have stayed on her own.

"Now, that's what I call an interesting development. My men and I won't have to wait until we reach the next town to get what we need after all." Farmon gave what she imagined was supposed to be a smile. Between the glint in his eyes and the wound splitting his cheek, it looked more like an evil grimace. "But I think I will be the first to plough that sweet little furrow of yours. That way I'll show you what I can do firsthand. You didn't want to watch me with one of the whores, so you'll no doubt be relieved."

The ice that had replaced Eyja's blood turned to fire. He meant to have her and then hand her over to the rest of his men. Over her dead body! She still had her dagger hidden in her boot. As soon as he came over her, she would bury it into his back.

"I won't lie down for you or any of your foul friends, so you can forget about it!" she spat, making to rush past him. She had to get to Moon now.

But the man was too fast for her. He grabbed her by the elbow and pinned her against the nearest tree trunk, pressing her face against the rough bark. Desperately, she tried to free herself from his hold. Farmon only laughed.

"I suggest you keep your strength for later, *Eirik*. You'll need it," he whispered into her ear, leaning against her back. Eyja gagged when a foul smell reached her nostrils. "The men will be only too glad to see to your needs. Only I'm not quite sure they'll want to use their mouths on you, unlike that dim-witted Norseman. What is the man thinking, using his hand to make himself come when there's a hot woman lying spread open in front of him? I won't be making the same mistaken, you can be sure of—"

A cry interrupted the terrible declaration. "Farmon? You have to come see this!"

Thank the gods. His friends needed him.

He pressed himself harder against her and she felt him stiff and hot against the small of her back. Bile rose in her throat. Thus far she had been aroused and flattered when feeling the proof of a man's arousal because they had been men she desired as well. With Farmon it made her want to vomit.

"We'll march today, as planned. While we do, I will enjoy telling my men the truth one by one, inform them of what delights awaits them at the end of the day. And then once we stop, you will spread your legs for us and give us the reward we deserve for ensuring your and your lover's safety."

Despite knowing she would never succeed in freeing herself, Eyja tried to push him away and only managed to scrape her cheek further against the tree bark. He was not budging an inch. "You think I will just let you—"

"Yes, you will. Because if you don't, my friends and I will take our revenge on your little 'cousin'. It won't be pretty. He's strong, I'll give him that, but there is only one of him and there are eight of us."

Eight of them. Yes. Eight men who would each want a turn with her, or more. She would not make it out of it unscathed. But Moon would hardly just watch as they each violated her in turn. Whether she protested or not, he would defend her, and then he would be killed, because he would not stop until he was dead. It was too late to save either of them.

What had she done? By provoking Moon she had signed both their death warrants. A sob escaped her lips. Farmon let out a grunt, evidently satisfied with her reaction. She guessed that for him, half the pleasure lay in letting her torture herself over what was to come. The actual possession tonight would be the crowning moment in a day of cruel anticipation.

"Think, while we walk, and then you will see that there is no choice. Tonight, we will have you."

Eyja was avoiding him.

Moon's chest tightened. He'd guessed—nay, dreaded—this would happen. After what he'd done to her, she would most probably not know how to behave with him. Everything had been altered by one moment of madness. She would now think him unhinged and depraved at best, too forceful at worst. What had possessed him to get between her legs in such a way? Back at the village if she had accused him of not considering her like a woman he would have laughed, and pointed out that she had only herself to blame for it, as she had done her best to ensure he did not. A few days ago even, he would have been able to let the provocation pass. But today... He had jumped at the chance of showing her she was wrong. It was new but he definitely did see her as a woman now.

And with his forceful demonstration, he'd embarrassed her.

Knowing she would not dare draw attention to them by refusing to have him walk next to her the way they usually did, he drew closer to her. As he'd expected, she didn't send him away, but she didn't acknowledge his presence by word or deed. For a while they walked in silence. Despite the foggy, gloomy morning, Farmon was more cheerful than usual and a few of his men seemed to share in his merriment. Moon shrugged. In all probability the prospect of a night of debauchery in the next town was responsible for their buoyant mood. The less he thought about what they would do with the poor women, the better.

This time Eyja did not seem to notice or care what the Saxons were talking about. She walked with her head down and the same focus she'd had when they had marched to York. If he didn't know better, he would have thought she was heading to her doom once again.

"Imp, I'm sorry. I should never have done that. I don't know what came over me."

Moon sighed. Here he was again, apologizing to her for being unable to control himself. The last time he had let his temper get the better of him, this time it was his lust. And he was making a mess of his apology, for he had made it sound as if he had no idea why *she* could possibly have provoked his desire. It would not surprise him if she sent him to hell.

But to his surprise, she actually answered, even if she didn't look at him.

"Don't be sorry. I was the one who pushed you."

"That is no excuse. I should not have—"

A noise in the undergrowth caused Eyja to turn her face to him. He hissed in shock when he saw that her right cheek was scratched and bruised. What was that? She'd been fine this morning when he'd left her.

"What happened to you?"

He barely stopped himself from reaching out and stroking her cheek. Tears flooded her eyes at the question, causing a new wave of alarm to crash through him. What *had* happened? Had she been attacked? But when? By whom? No one had joined their little group, no one had even be seen.

"'Tis nothing. After you left me this morning I-I walked into a tree," she stammered. "In this fog, I didn't see where I was going."

Walked into a tree? Moon blinked. Did she really expect him to believe that? For one, it hadn't been foggy that morning in the meadow, and even if it had, it would not have been enough to hide a twenty-foot tree standing right in front of her. Unless, of course, she had been so upset and disorientated by what had just happened between them that she had not paid attention to what she was doing... He knew she had a tendency to get distracted.

Remorse mingled with worry, making his guts churn anew. Why had he not stayed with her, made sure she was all right instead of leaving her on her own after such a momentous event? He had thought it best to give her a moment to compose herself but obviously it had been a mistake.

"We need to leave," she said before he could apologize again for doing the opposite of what he should have done. It was quickly becoming a habit, one he was not proud of. "I don't want to travel with Farmon and the others anymore."

The abrupt declaration caused him to stiffen and reevaluate his first impression. Had he gotten it wrong? Was the reason for Eyja's strange behavior fear rather than embarrassment? Was her altercation with Farmon earlier that morning responsible for her unease? Perhaps she dreaded the Saxon punishing her for the way she had challenged him, with good reason, because he wouldn't put it past the vile man to do just that. Or was it even worse? Had she noticed a change in the men's attitude toward her? He had not seen anything, but her feminine instinct would have picked up on the slightest change and she might worry about the possible consequences. If they'd heard her moans this morning then it wouldn't be long before they saw that all was not as it should be with his "cousin." He distinctively remembered her whimpers when pleasure had overcome her. It had been the sweetest sound but, undoubtedly, it had not been wise to indulge in such activities with the men lurking so near.

Well, if she had noticed something, he had better heed her warning. Eyja was a highly intuitive woman.

There was safety in numbers and he would have preferred to travel in a group but if that group was made up of men who could turn into a danger at any time, then they were better off taking their chances on their own. He'd had enough of Farmon and his cronies anyway.

"I agree," he said eventually, grateful for the fact that they could converse in a language no one around them understood. It made it easier to be private. "We'll just tell them we want to—"

"No. We can't let them suspect we're leaving." Eyja sounded panicked at the thought of confronting the men. He frowned. This was unusual. She was no coward. In fact, he would not have been surprised to see her march straight to the men and tell them she was done with their boorish ways. Something was definitely amiss.

"Why do you not want to—"

Another, louder rustling in the undergrowth had them all stopping again and looking around. Was a band of ruffians about to attack them? Moon groaned. That was the last thing he needed right now! Just when he'd started to think he might well be able to bring Eyja home in one piece, they were set upon.

Well, the men, whoever they were, would have a hard time bringing him down. He was pumped up and ready to go.

No sooner had he withdrawn one of his axes out of its sheath than a sounder of boars, at least twenty strong, erupted through the bushes, scattering the men. Everyone started to flee to avoid the wild animals, who, being accompanied by their young, would not hesitate to charge if they felt under threat. Moon took Eyja by the hand and led her away from the mayhem. This was their chance to leave the Saxons without any explanation. The propitious interruption would give them the head start they needed. By the time the company was whole again, they would be far enough away to hide. The fog would help as well, and tonight, they would be free.

Yes, this was their best, perhaps their only chance to give the men the slip without any unnecessary bother.

"Come. Now is the perfect time to lose Farmon and his friends."

He didn't need to say more. Eyja started to run, her hand still clasped in his. Such was her agility and speed that he had difficulty keeping up. After a while, she slowed down. "Wait. We had better climb up a tree."

"What? Why? There's no need." The boars were nowhere to be seen. They were safe.

But Eyja shook her head. "When the men start looking for us, they won't think of looking up. Between the foliage and the fog, they will never see us, it will be as if we had vanished into thin air."

It wasn't a bad idea, and he knew she climbed trees as well as any squirrel. Perhaps they should hide in the trees. Just then, as if to help him make a decision, they heard a shout in the distance.

"Halfdan? Eirik? Where are you? The boars are gone. You can come back."

Without a word, Eyja started to climb the nearest tree. He followed, doing his best to remain silent. A moment later they heard two men's voices.

"Where the devil have they gone? I don't care if we never see the Norseman again but I'm not letting that 'cousin' of his slip away before I've had a good poke at what she's hiding between her legs."

"Well, you'll have to wait for your turn. I'll go first and I guarantee it will be a long while before I'm satisfied."

Moon barely repressed a curse. Damnation, he'd been right! They knew. Of course, they did. Now that they had time to pay attention instead of blindly marching as fast as they could, they would have seen that "Eirik" was much more than a frail youth. He placed his hand over Eyja's in silent support. He could all too well imagine what it would do to her to hear the men talk so blithely about raping her.

When they walked under the tree the two Saxons didn't

even slow down. Moon stole a glance toward Eyja. She was hugging the tree trunk, trembling, and no wonder. The fate the men had in store for her was terrible. It made no doubt that all of them would have wanted a "poke," and there were eight of them, each more crude and dangerous than the next. She would never have gotten out of the ordeal unscathed, both physically and mentally.

As for him, he would not have made it either. He would have been killed, pure and simple, when he'd jumped to her aid. At one against eight, he wouldn't have stood a chance.

"That's why you wanted to leave, is it not?" he whispered once the men's voices had died down. It was exactly as he'd thought. As a woman, she would be used to seeing men look at her with desire in their eyes and would have recognized the signs he'd missed.

She nodded, her eyes huge with fright.

"Don't worry." He placed a hand over hers again, wishing he could do more. "I swear they will not touch a hair on your head."

All they had to do now was wait. The Saxons would search a while but would sooner or later admit defeat and head toward the nearest town.

Once night had fallen and the moon was up, they finally dared to climb down from their perch.

As soon as they touched the ground, Moon engulfed Eyja into his arms. He'd fought the need to do so for too long and he could not contain himself any longer. After the fright she'd just suffered, she needed it. Hell, *he* needed it too. Besides, there was no need to pretend anymore. Away from strangers, they could behave as a man and a woman behaved, and not worry about what others would think. To his relief, she melted against him. He sighed.

Peace was restored.

"Here, Imp, it's over," he said, speaking into her hair. "From now on, everything will be all right. We're safe, we're on our own, and soon we will be home."

CHAPTER EIGHT

That night, too worried they hadn't put enough distance between them and Farmon's men, neither Eyja nor Moon dared to sleep. So as to be able to spot any intruders approaching from a distance, they chose to set up camp up a nearby hill, one with a commanding view of their surroundings. The moon obliged them by shedding enough light for them to see the landscape all around.

They were as safe as they could be. No one would ambush them this night.

"Máni is obviously pleased with us bathing in the moonlight the other day and has decided to help us see our enemies as a reward for our respect," Moon observed wryly. Indeed in this light, any moving shadow would be immediately spotted and, thanks to the high position, any sound betraying the approach of a company of men would rise to their ears. Not that he expected any attacks. The Saxons would most likely not give chase now, but you never knew.

It was better to be safe than sorry.

"Yes," Eyja agreed. "'Tis good."

She did not quite join in the jest about the god of the moon but at least she answered, the brave little imp. He gave her hand a squeeze. She'd been badly shaken by their narrow escape. "Come. Let us sit."

Thanks to the warm temperature they didn't need to light a fire that would give them away. After eating the dried meat and bread they'd bought during their last halt, they sat back to back, each looking out in a different direction and providing the other one support. All night they saw and heard nothing, not even a deer or a boar. It seemed they had made it.

Once a timid sun pierced through the trees, Moon stood up to stretch and decreed that Eyja should try and get some sleep.

"I can keep guard on my own now. It will be much easier in the daylight, as I will be able to spot any traveler from miles around," he argued, taking in the purple shadows under her eyes. "'Tis safe for you to rest a moment. You need it." He almost added that it was an order before remembering that this was the surest way to make her bristle. Gentle persuasion was the way to go with her. "You'll feel better afterward."

Without a word, Eyja sat back down. That she didn't even argue showed him how right he'd been to insist. The poor woman was exhausted.

"All right, I will rest a moment. Then it will be your turn," she mumbled, curling to her side on the soft grass. He smiled to himself, remembering how he'd told her she slept like a woman. It had been no lie, and it was the most adorable sight.

"We'll see about me when you wake up. Just close your eyes."

He watched as she fell into a deep sleep, her curled fist by her head. Yes. Most definitely adorable. After a while, he decided he had better see what food he could find instead of ogling her and spotted a tangle of thorns some distance to his right. Blackberries. That was a start. They could find more food at the next farm they passed.

Eyja only woke up when the sun was at its zenith. Immediately, she let out a gasp and threw him an accusing glare. Although he'd fully expected that reaction, Moon couldn't help a smile. How wonderful to know someone so well you could predict what they would do or say.

"Half the day is gone! Why did you let me sleep for so long?"

He shrugged. "You needed it and we're in no hurry after all. The king is no longer here to force us to march like Roman legionaries."

"No, I suppose not..." she conceded slowly. "Did you get any sleep?"

He had not. Too intent on making sure no one was coming, he had not even thought of closing his eyes, instead scanning the horizon and gathering as many blackberries as he could in large leaves. He nodded toward the one he had placed next to her. "Don't worry about me," he grumbled, feeling suddenly weary.

"So you did not." She popped a few berries into her mouth and chewed. "Well, get some sleep now. I'll keep watch."

"I'm fine."

"You don't *look* fine," she said, standing up

"Eyja..." The imp was sorely trying his patience, and this when his temper was already short. "I just want to go, and we need to find more food. Sleep can wait."

"Very well."

To his surprise, she didn't argue but picked up the leaf full of berries and followed him. For once, though, he would actually have liked her to be her usual contrary self. If she had insisted, he might have allowed himself to be persuaded, for, in truth, after a night of constant vigil, he was exhausted and, as he'd just said, they were in no hurry. A nap would have been welcome.

In any case, they were off now. Surely he would be fine once he had eaten.

Just as they reached the bottom of the hill, Eyja came to a halt.

"Wait, I have a stone in my shoe." She sat on the ground to remove the soft leather boot and shook her head in consternation. "So many blisters... My poor feet. They are swollen and throbbing something fierce."

"No surprise there," Moon grumbled. They had been walking nonstop for days. By the time they made it back to the village, their shoes would be damaged beyond repair.

"There's a river just behind the trees. Do you mind if I go dip my feet in the water a moment? The cold might help to ease the worst of the pain."

"Of course not." How could he refuse?

"Thank you. Just wait for me here, I won't be long."

As soon as he sat on the soft grass, Moon knew he would fall asleep. He would not be able to resist the torpor invading his body while he waited. The only solution would have been to set off again, but he could not ask Eyja to put her boots back on when her feet were hurting. What harm could it do if he closed his eyes a moment? It had now been more than a day since they had parted company with Farmon and his men. If they were to find them, they would have already. Besides, Eyja would be on the lookout for anything suspicious and she was well within calling distance. The sun was warm on his skin, his eyelids were so heavy.

He lay on his back. Maybe he could just...

When he opened his eyes again, a reddish sun was hanging low over the horizon.

He sat bolt upright. Damn it all, the day was almost gone!

He got up and went in search for Eyja. She was sitting with her feet dangling in the water, her head tilted up to the sky.

Moon took a moment to admire the sight. The dying sun set her hair ablaze and made her skin glow. Right now it was impossible to imagine that woman had ever been in danger or in pain. She seemed so at peace, so at one with the nature around her.

So beautiful.

He cleared his throat. What was he doing, admiring her thus? At the noise he made, she turned to him. "Ah. Moon. Feeling better?"

The way she asked the question made his eyes narrow in suspicion. She sounded too satisfied by far and the hint of a smile was floating on her lips.

"There was no pebble in your shoe, was there?" he asked, suddenly certain she had only feigned compliance when he'd decided to set off, and then tricked him into getting the rest he needed by pretending to be hurt. She'd known a tired man would not be able to resist the lure of the soft grass.

"Not this time." She reddened, as if knowing he would not like to hear she'd lied. He did not, even if he wasn't as irate as he'd expected. Getting some sleep had done wonders for his mood, it seemed, and he was more grateful than anything else.

"I bet your foot isn't even blistered."

"Not yet," she admitted. "But there is a hole in my sole so it might be very soon. And the dip in the water did do me a lot of good. I also found some mushrooms and nuts, so we will be able to eat something before we set off."

He grunted and planted himself in front of her, helping her back to her feet. "Imp. I believe you are trying to take care of me."

"I believe I am." She gave a tentative smile and lifted her head to him. "And after all you've done for me I think it's the least I can do, don't you?"

Perhaps. But it did warm him nonetheless. Now he would have to add caring and considerate to the list of qualities the woman already possessed. If it carried on that way he might think her the most well-endowed woman of his acquaintance. Used to his mother's loving, supportive behavior at home growing up, Moon had long since decided that he would only ever settle with someone who could be such a mother to his children. But it was surprisingly hard to find someone whose idea of family life coincided with his amongst younger women. That was one of the reasons why he was in no hurry to start looking for a wife.

And now, Eyja was revealing herself to be more mature than he had given her credit for. Underneath the wild, untamed exterior was a protector. The thought made him smile. Some protector she made, being so small compared to him... And yet he never felt better than with her by his side. He knew he could rely on her, whatever the challenge facing them. Hadn't she been the one thinking to climb a tree to escape the Saxons? Hadn't she just ensured he got the rest he needed? What she lacked in strength she made up for in cunning and determination. In that way, as in so many others, they complimented one another perfectly.

"Come then, let's eat those mushrooms you prepared. Then we'll try to find a farm while there is still some daylight left and persuade the people to give us some bread and cheese."

Eyja giggled. "I will leave the persuading to you, if you don't mind. That way we'll both eat like royalty."

"What is that supposed to mean?"

"Don't tell me you haven't noticed how you seem to charm everyone, especially women?" She looked incredulous. But, yes, he had noticed. He just didn't think *she* had. So what did that mean? Had she been watching him interact with women? He didn't know what to make of the idea.

They sat down to eat the food Eyja had prepared while he slept. The mushrooms cooked over the fire were delicious, and there was a fair amount of shelled nuts to accompany them, but after his meager meal in the morning, Moon was ravenous. Fortunately they did find a farm just around the riverbend, and the farmer's wife was only too happy to swap one of their cumbersome axes for a whole loaf of bread and a generous serving of cheese. Winking, she added a couple of honey tarts for good measure, then looked at the purple horizon.

"'Tis dark already. I'm thinking you might prefer to bed in the stable at the back of the hut than in the forest."

Moon thanked her, doing his best to pretend not to see the blatant invitation in her eyes. If she had her way, he would not lie down in a bed of straw next to Eyja tonight, but atop her, and there would not be much sleeping.

"Thank you, mistress, but we'll be on our way now." He bowed. "Your concern honors you, but we are used to traveling at night."

"What's the matter?" Eyja asked as they hastened away with their food. "The farmer's wife was not to your tastes?"

"No one's wife is to my taste," he replied, biting off a piece of cheese. As a matter of principle, he had never bedded a married woman—that he knew of. Besides, how could she think he would leave her unprotected while he rutted away with a stranger? He was staying with her, and that was that. "Let's stop here," he decided, stopping at the foot of a mighty oak.

They ate the rest of the food in companionable silence and settled for a good night's sleep on the soft moss. High above in the sky, the stars were twinkling through the tree branches. Fortunately, for he didn't feel like getting a fire going, it was warm again. Despite his earlier nap, he could already feel his eyes closing.

"Tomorrow we'll avoid getting too close to the town," he said, whispering in the silence.

Eyja did not answer, but he knew she would have understood his way of thinking. Farmon and his cronies had made no secret of their intentions. They were headed for the nearest stew house, which would most probably be in town. It would not do for them to run into the disgruntled Saxons when they were itching for a tumble and vexed by their sudden disappearance.

"Yes," she said eventually. "We need not hurry, but I would like to reach home before the week is out."

Three days later, they came into view of their local town.

Nestled at the bottom of the hill, a familiar, comforting sight with its squat church planted in the middle of the low wooden houses, it was perhaps half a day's walk away. Tomorrow at the latest they would be home. The village lay just on the other side of the forest. Eyja had the impression she'd been gone for months, when in reality it had been a little over two weeks. In that short length of time she'd accumulated enough experiences to last her a lifetime and she could not wait to get back to less dangerous surroundings, even if she was not sure things would ever be the same. She felt changed beyond all recognition by what she had gone through. There had been the battle with Hardrada's men, of course. The horrors she had witnessed that day had transformed her into a different person, but that was not all.

More importantly, what Moon had done to her on the forest floor had made her a different woman.

"Here we are," he said, coming to a halt. "Home. How do you feel?"

"Relieved."

"Mm. I bet." Moon pursed his lips as he surveyed the familiar view. "It looks... different somehow."

She nodded, knowing exactly what he meant. "Yes. As if we'd left for years rather than days."

"Exactly."

Of a common accord, they stopped in the woods for the night, instead of hurrying to try to reach the town gates before sunset. Eyja was grateful for the delay, as she didn't feel ready to be parted from Moon just yet. As soon as they entered the village, they would be assaulted by friends and family demanding to hear their story, showering them with questions. There would be few opportunities to see him. After two weeks spent by his side night and day, she wasn't sure how she would handle it, even if, admittedly, they already spent more time together than the average friends.

Once they'd eaten the now customary roasted rabbit, Moon stretched his long body next to her and cradled the back of his head in his entwined fingers.

"I don't know if I'm looking forward to going back to the village, you know," he mused, his gaze on the sky up above. The stars had started to come out, piercing the night with their flickering light. So fragile, yet so beautiful.

"Oh?" Eyja's heart started to beat a fierce rhythm. Surely he didn't mean he wanted to accompany her home and then set off again on a new adventure? She would hate that. She needed him in her life. "Why not?"

A sigh. "What do you think? Your father is going to skin me alive for allowing you to march with the army. And that's before he finds out about what we—"

"He's never going to find out about that because I'm not going to tell him!" she cut in fiercely. Did he really imagine that she would want to tell her father, of all people, that a man had buried his face between her thighs? She would die of mortification before she even finished the sentence. "It's got nothing to do with him. What do you take me for?"

He pierced her with a stare. In the firelight his eyes glowed like gems.

"I'm not sure I can answer that question. I don't know what to take you for anymore, Imp. I'm not sure either of us are the same people we were when we set off for war."

Ah, so he didn't have the intention to travel the land, he only felt the same as she did, unsettled and unsure about how to handle a return to normality. It reassured her. She would have hated to know she was the only one feeling altered by what had happened between them. But one thing was for sure, whatever life she was to have now, she still wanted Moon to be a part of it.

"What we are for one another is something *we* will have to decide, no one else."

He grunted, which could have meant that he agreed with her or that he had no idea how they were to manage to do such a thing. In truth, she had no idea either.

"I think it's time for a change," she mused, lying down herself.

Moon turned to face her, curious. "You mean you would leave the village?"

"No." It made her smile that he thought the same thing she had thought a moment ago about him. But she was not going anywhere. The village had never appeared dearer to her now that she had spent time away from it. "Only that I should perhaps leave my parents' hut."

All her brothers had left a while ago, even if only Steinar was married. At one and twenty, wasn't it time she did the same? But where would she go? She could not think of a single empty hut that could become hers. Could she ask her father to build one for her? Would he agree to have her leave if it was not to start a family with a husband? That was the usual reason women left the family home.

Yes, it was, but everyone knew she was not the usual

woman. Her cropped hair as well as her presence in the woods here tonight attested to that.

"Well, if you really mean it, I could help." Moon cut through her musings.

Her heart skipped a beat. Was he offering to have her come live with him? Surely not? True, he lived in his own, so no one would object to her moving in if he decided to have her, but...

"What do you mean? How could you could help?"

"With the building of a new hut, of course."

He winked at her and she groaned. How wrong could one be? He had not meant to welcome her under his roof at all. Of course not, how stupid was she for even entertaining the notion? Not only did friends not live together, but what would he do with her when he brought a conquest home if she was in the hut? She grimaced at the thought. Now that she knew just how skilled and generous he was in bed, she could not help a pang of jealousy at the idea of the next lucky woman who would enjoy his attentions.

He mistook her reaction for offence. "Ah, don't tell me. You actually wanted to build the hut yourself, is that what it is? I wouldn't put it past you, you know."

Eyja shrugged. Was it such a bad idea?

"I'm sure I could build a hut, if I really put my mind to it. After all, I have a head to work out what is to be done and two arms to chop and carry wood, just like any man. I'm no expert, but I don't think the part that I *don't* have," she added, staring pointedly at his groin, "has any role to play in the building of a house?"

Moon gave a throaty laugh that sent goosebumps all the way to her toes and shook his head. "No. None whatsoever."

CHAPTER NINE

In the end, it was not just Wolf who pounced on Moon. It was a whole pack of them. All three of Eyja's brothers, who happened to be repairing the roof of their parents' hut when they approached the village, spotted them from a distance and fell on him as soon as he reached the well.

"You maggot!" Steinar, her eldest brother, and even bigger than their massive father, was the first to speak. "I'm going to make you wish you'd never—"

"Shut your mouth, Steinar!" Eyja barked, a true she-wolf herself. Knowing she had nothing to fear for her brother would never touch her, however irate he was, she placed herself between the two men. "None of this is Moon's fault. I decided to leave and join the army on my own. This has nothing to do with him."

"I don't care who made you go in the first place! He should have dragged you back home by the skin of your ass as soon as he realized what you were doing! Does he have no sense?"

Her second brother, Torsten, sounded even more furious. Perhaps because up until then they had been best friends and he had expected more from him. Moon could understand the feeling. He would be furious himself if Torsten had allowed one of his sisters to place herself in danger. And he had to admit it did look bad. No one had seen them leave separately, yet here they were, coming back together. It did appear as if they had been in agreement all along. No one would believe his claim that he had not played any role in her decision, for what woman chose to go to war when nothing forced her to?

"He was furious when he saw I had joined the men and told me I should go back. I refused and so he did everything he could to protect me," Eyja stood her ground, the foolish imp.

A surge of gratefulness burst through him because, though once again she was speaking when she should perhaps have stayed silent, she was defying her beloved brothers for him. Before he could think, he placed a hand on the small of her back in a silent thank you. As soon as he saw Torsten's eyes narrow, he knew it had been a mistake. He took his hand away as calmly as he could, but it was too late, the damage had been done.

"If he touched you, I swear I—"

"*If* he'd touched me, it would be none of your business," Eyja retorted.

That, without a doubt, had been the wrong thing to say. This time he could not help but wish she had kept her mouth closed. All three men glared at him and Moon knew he was going to have to fight his way out of this. He would not die, because the three brothers would not dare kill him outright, but he would most likely suffer for days. Bones might well be broken. Oh well, that was no more than he had expected.

He lifted his chin, ready for it.

"Come on, then, fight me if it will make you feel better. My conscience is clear."

Sven, the third and youngest brother, took Eyja by the arms to stop her from intervening while Steinar and Torsten planted themselves in front of him. They were impressively tall but so was he. They were more muscular than him, but he knew he was quicker. They were blinded by rage, but he was calm, and able to think clearly. Perhaps he could actually inflict some damage before he went down. If Sven stayed out of it, too busy holding Eyja off, he might stand a chance.

Steinar threw the first punch. Moon parried easily but could not avoid the blow to the ribs delivered by Torsten a heartbeat later. That was the problem with fighting two men at the same time. You could not be everywhere at once. He doubled over and heard Eyja cry out.

"Stop it, stop!" She sounded on the verge of a fit of a fit "He's done nothing wrong!"

Loath to have her see such a spectacle, he kicked Steinar, then swung his fist at Torsten, who howled in rage and pain combined when the blow landed on his temple. Perhaps his determination would be enough to give the brothers pause. He didn't think they actually wanted to kill him, despite their anger, so they might retreat when they saw he was not going to go down as easily as they had hoped.

"Enough."

That one word caused everyone to still. Wolf was walking toward them, followed by his wife, Merewen, who threw herself into Eyja's arms. The two women started crying, alleviating some of the tension between the men. Moon straightened back up and was able to catch his breath. Now at least he would be able to present his version of events to a man who would listen instead of using his fists.

Wolf was the village leader, a fair and measured man. With luck he would see the situation for what it was.

"Halfdan. A word with you."

Halfdan.

Moon's heart fell to the pit of his stomach at the use of his real name. As far back as he remembered, the Icelander had only ever called him Moon. Now he was in real trouble. Wouldn't it have been better to face the beating the three brothers were itching to inflict on him than follow Eyja's father to his hut? The confrontation would be tense. Calm as he appeared to be, it was clear the man was beside himself with fury. Fair and measured as he was in his dealings with everyone, this was different. The fact that it involved his only daughter meant he would not be able or willing to remain as detached as usual.

The village leader would have given him a fair hearing.

The family man might not be as well disposed.

After one last glance in Eyja's direction, Moon set off after Wolf, who'd already started to walk to his hut. No sense in making things even more difficult for himself by keeping him waiting.

Once inside the hut, his heart plummeted further. It was not empty. His father was standing by the window, his face set in granite. Word of his return had apparently spread, which was not surprising, given the fact that it had been followed by a fight in the middle of the village.

Faced with the two most formidable men he knew, who were more like brothers than friends to each other, men he had always looked up to, men he liked and respected, Moon felt like a child. It was an unpleasant feeling to say the least for a man of eight and twenty.

For a long moment no one spoke. It was clear the men were waiting for him to start and explain himself, if he dared. He did dare, because he had done nothing wrong.

"I understand your anger," he started, straightening himself to his full height. "But I swear I had no hand in Eyja's decision to join King Harold's army. I know now that she overheard my conversation with Torsten and decided to join as well, but I was unaware of it at the time, as she didn't tell anyone."

He imagined that Torsten was how the villagers had figured out what had happened to her. Upon hearing about Eyja's disappearance, his friend would have relayed their conversation to her father, and his intentions to join the army.

It did look as if they had left together, and Moon had no idea how he was to convince Wolf that they had not.

"I only found out what she had done on the evening of the first day, when it was already too late to send her back. We were too far from home at this point and she would have had to travel alone. I doubt she would have heeded my orders anyway, you know how stubborn she is. So I decided it was safer to keep her by my side and let it be known she was my cousin."

"Yes. It was much safer to take her to the midst of a battle to the death, and keep her amongst thousands of violent men." Wolf was not impressed.

Moon raised both his hands in surrender. "What else could I do? I could not abandon her. We all know she would have followed the army anyway if her decision was made, regardless of what I said. Your daughter is one opinionated woman. I thought that way at least I could keep an eye on her."

To his relief, the men did not contradict him. Evidently they had the honesty to agree that it was impossible to stop Eyja once she had set her mind to something.

"Why did you want to join the army in the first place?" his father roared, his temper finally exploding. "Why would you choose to fight against your own people?"

Moon had known the question would come, and he was ready for it. He took in a deep breath.

"*Faðir*, with all due respect, these invaders are not my people." He'd struggled hard enough with his conscience, he was not going to let anyone make him feel guilty now that it was all over. "They came to pillage, conquer and kill. The people in my village, my people, are nothing like that, *you* are nothing like that. You all came here peacefully in search of a new life, to settle and mingle with the local population. Mother was born here, and so was I. It is our home and I wanted to defend it." He paused, knowing that mentioning his mother could only soothe his father's temper. And indeed his fury seemed to abate somewhat. "I heard all about the raids happening many years ago. I could not stand idle and watch the country I love being torn apart again, I had to do something. I did and we won. We sent the raiders back. I am proud to have helped, in some small way, to spare so many lives."

The light in his father's eyes told him he understood his thinking and was no longer offended. At any other time, he might well have congratulated him on his decision. Even better, Wolf seemed to share the sentiment.

Moon decided to push his advantage. Perhaps this would not be a total disaster.

"Being born of a Saxon and an Icelander and having seen that our two peoples could live side by side in harmony, Eyja felt the same. She did place herself in danger but it was for a good cause. She was brave, like any man in that army, and you should be proud of her. Her contribution was crucial and she was not even injured. We won and she is safe. That is all that matters, is it not?"

For a long moment neither men spoke. But the tension in the hut had eased visibly.

"What about you, son? Were you hurt?" his father asked, allowing his gaze to wander over him.

"A mere cut to the thigh, nothing worth mentioning. I've already forgotten about it."

Wolf nodded, as if satisfied. "Very well. I have only one more question." Moon stilled, sensing this would be the toughest question yet. And he had a feeling he knew what it would be. "Did you two lie together?"

"No."

It wasn't hard to sound convincing, since the Icelander obviously meant: Did you possess her? and he had not. All the same, he felt a twinge of guilt, because even if it was true that he had not entered Eyja's body or taken her innocence, he had most definitely wanted to do it, and he *had* been intimate with her. So intimate he could still taste her on his tongue, a maddening thing. Since when did he obsess about a woman's taste days after he'd pleasured her with his mouth?

Wolf held his gaze, evidently trying to assess his good faith. Moon did his best not to flinch or look away. For good measure, he almost added that he would never have bedded a woman he saw as a sister, but he did not, because... Well, because unfortunately, he did not see Eyja in that way anymore. As to how he saw her, he wasn't so sure.

But, as she'd said last night, that was something for them to figure out, no one else.

Slowly, Wolf nodded and took a step back.

Moon exhaled in relief. He'd made it. He'd convinced the Icelander he had done the best he could have in the circumstances, and escaped retribution. Eyja's three brothers would not dare lay a hand on him now that their father had concluded he did not need to be punished. He was safe.

"Thank you, Wolf," he said sincerely, understanding how worried the man would have been for his only daughter's safety. If he had a daughter one day, he would react in the same way.

"I will need a word with my reckless daughter now, obviously, but you're free to go."

Moon turned toward the door.

Before he could reach the handle, it burst open and Eyja entered the hut, eyes blazing.

"Don't you dare punish Moon, *Faðir!*" she cried out before anyone could say anything. "He didn't do anything wrong.

None of it is his fault. I wanted to go, and I didn't tell anyone! He found me when it was too late, and he was furious, but still he protected me all the way to York and back, pretended I was his cousin so no one would bother me and even bought an axe for me. He did all he could do to—"

"Are you quite finished?" Wolf interrupted, sounding amused in spite of himself.

Eyja blinked. Was her father *amused*? She dared not hope it was the case. What was going on? She had expected him to be irate at the very least. But he seemed calm and, most importantly, Moon seemed whole. There was no blood on his clothes, no torn limbs lying on the floor. Her breathing eased somewhat. Then she saw that Sigurd was also here. Her chest tightened again. No doubt the Dane would hate her for putting his son in such a difficult position, with good reason. But he wasn't glaring at her or even swearing. She took heart from that.

Perhaps against all odds she and Moon would get away unscathed.

"The boy's explained what pushed you both into this foolish enterprise. It was brave of you to want to defend your mothers' country and Sigurd and I commend you for it. He told us that he had no hand in your decision, which I all too easily believe but would like you to confirm." Her father's eyes had never been bluer, the expression on his face more forbidding. He was no longer amused but she stood her ground.

"No, I told you. He had no hand in my decision."

There was a pause. "He also promised he didn't touch you while you were gone. Is that the case?"

Her gaze met Moon's for the briefest moment and she couldn't help it. She blushed. Although she knew what her father meant—that they had not lain together as lovers—and she should have confirmed it unequivocally, she thought back to the moment in the forest when Moon had lapped at her like a starved beast. Oh, yes, he had most definitely touched her then. And she had loved it.

Her father's expression became thundery. "I see."

Moon took a step forward. "It's not what you—"

"Silence!" Wolf snarled, not even looking at him. Then he asked her, articulating every word. "Were you willing?"

It was only then that Eyja understood what she had unwittingly led her father to believe. All the blood drained from her veins. He thought Moon had taken advantage of the fact that they were away from home to press his unwanted advances onto her. "I... Yes, of course! I mean... As I said, nothing happened but if it had then, of course, I would have been wi—"

"Enough!" This time it was Sigurd who interrupted. "No son of mine would ever force a woman!" he roared, coming to face his oldest friend. "If I were in any doubt about that, I would cut off his balls myself, make no mistake about it." He glared at Moon, who had gone the color of whey at the prospect. Eyja could not help a grimace herself. The Beast had awoken. "No, I know he didn't rape her, but that doesn't mean I approve of what he did, taking advantage of a moment of vulnerability to get his way. It is not the honorable way to seduce a woman."

"That's not what happened!"

"He didn't do that!"

The two older men ignored her and Moon's protests and carried on staring at each other, their attitude reminiscent of two dogs taking the measure of one another before a fight. Would they actually come to blows? After a while the tension eased and it looked as if they had come to an understanding. They nodded in silent agreement and turned toward them slowly, ominously. The same determination was glowing in their eyes. They had reached a decision and would not be moved. Everything within Eyja tightened.

This would be terrible.

"We are going to wait until we know whether there is a child or not," Sigurd started.

A child! Now she was aghast. If they thought this was a possibility, then they really thought she and Moon had lain together, perhaps more than once. It was all her fault. She had allowed doubt to creep into their minds. "It's not—"

"And if there is one," her father finished, "then the two of you are going to marry and raise it together."

"But, *Faðir!*" she and Moon exclaimed at the same time, each looking at their own father.

For a moment neither man said a word. Then Wolf spoke. "There is nothing to discuss. I will not have my only daughter spurned and discarded by her selfish lover."

"And I will not have any grandchild of mine growing up without his cowardly father," Sigurd added. "Every child needs a family."

"But there is not going to be any child, that's what we're trying to say," Eyja cried out. Why weren't they listening?

"Let's hope not," her father said between his teeth.

"No, we mean, it's impossible that she be with child because we never lay together," Moon took a step forward, not looking at her. "I told you so."

"Yes, you did. And then I asked my daughter if you had touched her and she looked about to faint."

"That's because..." Eyja came to stand next to Moon. She was not going to be left out of this conversation, not when they were talking about her! "That is not the same question."

Moon threw her a furious stare. *What is wrong with you?* he seemed to say. *Stop talking now!*

Yes, she should, since apparently she couldn't seem to say any of the right things. Except... Nothing she could say now would make this worse. Her father was already convinced Moon was a liar, and she was now debauched and with child.

Sigurd agreed and wanted her to marry the man responsible for that sorry state of affairs. So what did she have to lose?

"I cannot be with child, as I am still a virgin," she said, squaring off her shoulders.

Despite the embarrassing nature of the claim, she somehow found the strength to look her father in the eye as she spoke because she knew she was telling the truth. He didn't appear the least convinced, however. He crossed his arms over his massive chest and looked down at her, making her feel like a ten-year-old girl.

"You cannot be with child because you're still a virgin," he said, as if this was the most ridiculous thing he'd ever heard.

"Yes."

"And I am to believe you without proof after what you did, I suppose? Sneaking out of the village in the dead of night, hiding your intentions, lying about your identity, and making your mother sick with worry in the process."

At the mention of her mother, Eyja knew she had lost the fight. Her father was a generous soul, and he would have forgiven much. He usually gave people the benefit of the doubt and was inclined to forgiveness. But there was one thing guaranteed to make someone get on his wrong side. It was hurting his beloved wife. The couple he formed with Merewen, the Saxon he had bought thirty years ago to spare her a terrible fate as a slave was an inspiration for many, none more so than their four children.

"Your mother barely slept for two weeks, imagining you dead or raped or lost or burned or drowned or cut in half or anything else you want to add to the list. And I, whose sole role in life is to ensure her happiness, could do nothing to ease her mind." He clenched his teeth, as if seeing his wife's anguish had caused him immense pain.

Sigurd placed a hand on his friend's shoulder, offering

support. "So we'll do as we said. We'll wait to see whether there is a child before we decide anything."

Eyja watched the two men walk over to the door. There would be no swaying them, so she stayed silent.

"You both can stay here a moment, while I go tell your brothers they are not to kill Halfdan just yet."

Not yet. The words made her shiver. Surely he would not have him killed?

Of course not. He was nothing if not fair in his dealings. In all her life, she had never seen him order anyone's execution, despite him having dealt with truly nasty individuals. And besides, she would soon bleed and be able to prove she was not with child, so there was nothing to fear. Moon would not die because of her and her big mouth.

"Your mother will want to see you as soon as you're allowed to come out," Sigurd said in his son's direction, as he followed his friend out of the hut. "Make sure you don't dally. She, too, got herself into a state thinking of all that could have happened to you and you had better apologize to her with all you have or you will be sorry. Forget about Eyja's brothers, *I* will be the one making you regret your actions."

There was nothing else to say.

The door closed and Eyja found herself on her own with Moon.

CHAPTER TEN

"What the *hell* was that?" Moon exploded, swiveling to face Eyja.

But she wasn't looking at him. She had sat down on a stool and was wringing her fingers, oblivious to his outburst.

"My own father... I can't believe he thought I was lying," she said to herself.

"Can't you?" he snorted. "Considering what you said and how you said it?"

No wonder the Icelander was convinced the two of them were lovers. The foolish imp had all but described what he had done to her in that forest. And this after promising she would not reveal what had happened! He could have punched a hole through the wall of the hut, such was his fury.

He forced himself to calm down. Eyja had not precisely said that they had lain together, their two fathers had reached that conclusion on their own. But how could they have done otherwise? Her reaction when asked if it was true he had not touched her had been just as damning as if she'd admitted out loud he had buried his face between her legs to feast on her. A child accused of stealing a honey tart and innocent of the crime will not convince anyone he didn't do it by hiding his hands behind his back because they happened to be stained with blackberry juice at the time.

"Couldn't you have used your judgement for once and kept your mouth shut?" he roared. "I was just about to walk out of there, having earned both our fathers' forgiveness for what we did, and you had to come in and ruin it all!"

He couldn't remember ever being so angry, even when he had found her amidst the army of Saxons, dressed as the least convincing boy he had ever seen. Why? Why was he so irate to be mistaken for her lover when he had not minded being accused of dragging her off to war, which surely could be seen as a much graver offence? He had no idea, and that didn't help him hold on to his composure.

Eyja finally looked up at him. The expression on her face was icy cold, and her eyes once again put him in mind of frost. "Oh so you do think I possess some judgement, even if in your opinion I never use it. I'm flattered."

His nostrils flared. She dared speak to him thus when he was already furious and *she* was in the wrong? It was not to be borne! "Don't even start. I'm not in the mood for—"

"Well, neither am I! And what are you angry for anyway?" she cut in, not in the least impressed by his show of anger. Damn it, he should have known. She had never been one to cower. "Are you so scared you might be forced to marry me? Don't worry. We both know that the threat is meaningless as I am not carrying your child. In a few days I will bleed and this will all blow over. It will be as if it had never happened."

This reasonable answer did little to appease him. "I would have preferred not to be seen as a liar, thank you very much," he hissed. "Even if it's just for a few days."

"Well, you should have thought of that before you lied and

claimed not to have touched me," Eyja snapped, standing up at last. "Because you did touch me. You did more than that. You put your finger inside me, you licked me until I—"

"All right, I did!" he roared. Really, did the woman have no sense of self-preservation? He was on the verge of an outburst and she was calling him a hypocrite and reminding him of what he had done to her. As if he had forgotten any of it! The feel of her tight sheath convulsing for him, the incredible hot softness, the taste of her pleasure... He already feared he would remember them until the day he died. "I did touch you. And it turned out to be the biggest mistake I ever made."

The silence following his declaration almost crackled.

"A mistake," she repeated in a deathly voice. "Well, I suppose I know where I stand, don't I?"

With those words she made for the door. He could tell from the way she walked that her legs were barely supporting her.

"Eyja, wait." He could not let her go like this, not when she looked mortally wounded, not after calling what he had done to her the biggest mistake he'd ever made. In truth, he did not see it that way.

She stopped but kept her back to him.

"Why should I wait? You are supposed to stay here until my father has instructed my brothers not to kill you, but I can go. They love me, they will not tear me limb from limb. I have nothing to fear, they will not hurt me." She threw him a look over her shoulder, superb in her disdain. "It's better if I leave, as I would hate for you to make any more *mistakes*."

A MISTAKE.

That's what Moon would think when he saw her now, how he would consider her for the rest of his life. Not as a childhood friend, not as an annoying imp, not as a woman, but as the biggest mistake he had ever made.

A sob building in her throat, Eyja went to find her mother, whom she expected to be in the vegetable patch at the back of the hut, her favorite place. This was not the homecoming she had hoped for or even imagined. Only this morning she and Moon had woken up side by side in the woods and shared a joke about the time he had dared her to eat a moldy apple. She had bitten into it and might well have eaten the rest if he'd not snatched the fruit from her hand with cries of horror. There had been such warmth in his voice when he'd told her he'd always admired her spirit that, for a moment, she had almost thrown herself into his arms and begged him to take her.

And now he might not want to see her again.

She found her mother shelling beans on the bench by the tree.

"What is it, sweetheart? Have you been crying?"

"I'm sorry," she sobbed, falling into her mother's arms. "I'm so sorry for leaving like this, for worrying you. It was not my intention. I only wanted to help, wanted to stop the invaders, do something that would make you proud. And then, when we arrived, I was so scared! I realized I had no idea what I was doing. But I didn't want to change my mind, not after having come all this way... And Moon, he— "

"I know." Her mother held her tighter, cutting her fumbled explanations short. "It's all right. I understand why you wanted to go, your father just explained it to me. I'm your mother, so I'll always be proud of you and I'm a Saxon, so I cannot help but be touched by the fact that you wanted to defend my country. And I'm glad you weren't on your own. Moon was the best man you could have had with you. He's strong and honorable, he will have protected you, and understood better than anyone else what your motivations were. You grew up together. He knows you inside out."

The innocent comment sent heat to Eyja's whole body. He *did* know her inside out now. Literally. His fingers, his tongue had explored her hidden depths. Yes. And he considered it the biggest mistake he had ever made.

As if that was not enough, he'd been told he would have to spend the rest of her life with her, precisely because of that mistake.

"*Faðir* said Moon and I would have to get married if I happened to carry his child, but... Moon will never want to marry me. He hates me."

"What are you talking about? He's never hated you."

"He does now, because this is all my fault. Because of me he will be saddled with a wife he didn't choose, a woman he doesn't love."

The biggest mistake of his life.

"Do you mean that you could be with child?"

Eyja stilled when she suddenly remembered that this was impossible and therefore a marriage between her and Moon would never come to pass. In her distress she had quite forgotten it. As consolations went, it was a small one.

"No. I cannot be, since we never lay together. I told *Faðir* as much but he didn't believe me."

A silence. Then a question, spoken in a tentative voice. "Did anything happen even if you didn't lie together? Your father would never have doubted you if he'd not gotten the impression there was something between you two."

Yes. That was the whole problem. Despite her promise to Moon not to mention what had happened, she had betrayed the new intimacy between them. Eyja bit her bottom lip. Could she confide in her mother? This was embarrassing. But she sensed she could have an ally and in that moment she desperately needed one. Someone who would know the truth and believe her. Someone who would not judge her. Her mother could be that person. The two of them had always been very close.

She took in a deep breath. "Yes, we... I mean, he—"

"My clothes!"

Ari, Hilda's son, appeared out of nowhere and skidded to a halt in front of her, his rolling eyes betraying his fury. Eyja's chest hollowed. Having to justify her theft—her *borrowing*, rather—of his clothes was the last thing she needed when she already felt so wretched.

"Forgive me. Ari, I—"

"You were the one who stole them, so you could go to war! I should have known."

"No, I didn't steal them, only I needed men's clothes and as you aren't as—" She stopped herself before she could offend Ari further by pointing out she'd chosen his clothes because he was quite frail for his age. Perhaps Moon had a point. She really needed to learn to curb her tongue and exercise better judgement. "Anyway, I always meant to give them back, I swear."

"Well, I don't want them back!" he cried, with as much disgust as if she'd offered to smother him in pig fat. "They're all ruined now."

Eyja swallowed. That was exactly what Moon had warned her of on the first night, when he'd found her. And right now she could not deal with it. Tears started to sting her eyes. Could this day get any worse? Would no one believe her, whatever she said?

"Ari," her mother soothed before she could start crying. "You're right. The clothes are quite ruined, so I will get you new braies and a new tunic, along with a nice leather belt to compensate you for the inconvenience. How would you like that?"

The youth was instantly appeased, and no wonder. His clothes had been rather tattered to begin with. "Very well."

"Wolf was telling me how glad he is that you helped our daughter to stay safe, even if indirectly. Thanks to the disguise you provided for her, she was able to pass unnoticed amongst the men, and keep out of harm's way. You have his eternal gratitude, and mine."

The mention of her father, whom everyone respected in the village, was a masterstroke of diplomacy, and sealed the deal. Now Ari would be able to boast to everyone he had earned the Icelander's approval by helping his daughter in some small way.

"Tell him if he needs anything else, I'm his man."

Without throwing so much as a glance in Eyja's direction, he walked away.

Once they were alone again, her mother placed a hand over her shoulder. "It's been a hard few weeks, physically and mentally, I bet. Go home, get washed and changed into your normal clothes, have something to eat and then rest. You will feel better in the morning for it."

Would she really? Eyja was not so sure, but she did feel drained, so she did not protest. At least in the hut, she would not walk into anyone wanting to shame or accuse her of some dark deed.

As she slipped back into her soft woolen dress, she could not contain the sob she'd been fighting. Here she was, dressed as a woman once again. It was as if everything was back to normal. Except she knew that it was not.

Everything had been turned on its head.

CHAPTER ELEVEN

"What have you done to Eyja?"

Guilt instantly sliced through Moon. What did Thorfinn know about the argument he'd had with Eyja? Had he overheard them argue yesterday in Wolf's hut? It was possible, after all, they had hardly been discreet. Anyone might have heard them shouting. Had he seen her cry when she'd left the hut? Or was he simply referring to the fact that they had gone to fight the Norsemen together? Was he, too, assuming that her brothers' friend had been the one leading her into danger? It was better to behave as if that was the reason behind his question.

He dropped his axe. The chopping of wood would have to wait. He'd hoped to ease some of his frustration by reducing the logs to kindling but it hadn't worked.

"If you mean I abducted her and forced her to go to battle with me, then you're mistaken. She was the one who chose to—"

"I'm not talking about that!" Thorfinn spat. "But you go away together for a few days and suddenly she doesn't want to be with me anymore. So what did you do?"

"She doesn't want to be with you?" Moon repeated stupidly,

heart thumping hard in his chest. Since when was Eyja "with" anyone? And what did the man mean by them going away together for a few days? He made it sound as if they had gone on a pleasure outing. They had not, they had gone to war. Eyja could have died, and he didn't seem to care. "Are you and Eyja involved?" he asked, unable to wait another moment to know what was going on.

There was another pause. "We... erm, shared a few private moments before she left."

Thorfinn was being diplomatic but Moon had no time for euphemisms. "You mean you slept together?" The question came out more like a growl.

If the man was surprised by his question or his tone, he didn't show it. "No. She wouldn't let me bed her, only... Never mind. All I'm saying is that now she doesn't even want to do that."

Do what exactly? The question was burning Moon's lips. He swallowed it back, with difficulty. Perhaps it was better he didn't know. But there was one thing he had to clarify. "You mean you went to her today to ask if you could resume your...?" He stopped, not quite knowing how to refer to it.

"I did. And a whole lot of good that did me. She refused."

The man was getting mightily aggrieved but Moon could feel his own temper about to explode. He was incredulous. They had only been back a day, Thorfinn knew Eyja had been through hell, fighting an army of invaders, was exhausted by walking to the other end of the country, and all he could do was to press her for attentions, attentions she clearly wasn't interested in, complain when she refused, and blame another man for her refusal.

"Mm, tell me, did you make her come when you shared those 'private moments'?" Perhaps talking in euphemisms was not such a bad idea after all. It helped to keep the worst images from his mind.

"Come?"

Thorfinn stared at him as if he'd spoken in a foreign tongue and Moon considered his question answered. He had not.

"Yes, come," he said dangerously. The notion that the man had not been able to offer her pleasure, had not even noticed or cared, was the worst thing he'd heard so far, which was saying something. "You know. Did she cry out your name in ecstasy? Did she grab at your hair to keep you closer? Did she beg for more?"

"She... She did ask for more."

"I bet she did." Because she hadn't had what she wanted. "Well, don't blame me if she doesn't want to get near you again. By the sound of things it's clearly not *my* fault. Ask yourself what you could have done to make her come back to you, ready for more."

With those words, he stormed away.

Thorfinn and Eyja were involved with one another... This he hadn't seen coming, and the idea disturbed him. Why? The man was no worse than any other in the village, in fact he was probably better than most. Despite his anger, Moon had the honesty to admit he was personable and attractive—to women at least. That must be why she had chosen him. But still he was disturbed by the notion. Was it because it bothered him that the man had not seen to her pleasure? Was it because that day in the forest he had thought to be the first one to touch her intimately? Yes, perhaps it had something to do with that.

But why had she not told him? She had let him assume she was new to all this.

Then he reflected that he had not mentioned his earlier conquests either. Why would she have thought it timely or even necessary to say she had already been in a man's arms? He knew she was fearless, wild at heart and she was already one and twenty. It stood to reason she would have wanted to experiment what could happen between a man and a woman.

But why had she refused to bed Thorfinn, who'd clearly seen her as a woman and been ready to give her what she wanted, and all but forced him to make love to her that day in the forest, when it had been clear he was fighting the urge to do it with all his might? Would he ever understand the workings of her mind? The imp seemed to be forever doing the thing least expected of her.

Yes, he should stop trying to make sense of it for fear of going mad.

He headed straight to the river, determined to do just that.

"It's true then. You went to fight Hardrada's men."

Eyja slowed down.

Bragi was loitering by the well with two of his awful friends. The miller's nephew had always been a bully, from the moment he'd been able to talk, but he'd only ever bothered with boys. Girls had been below his notice. As a grown man, he only spoke to women he wanted to take to his bed, and thankfully she'd not been one of them. He had never addressed her more than a perfunctory word.

And now he wanted to draw her into a conversation. Well, she was not going to indulge him.

She would have ignored the men and walked straight past them but one of his brawny friends placed himself directly in front of her, blocking her way. Eyja had no other choice but to stop.

An immense weariness invaded her. Would she forever be met with obstacles and problems?

Earlier that morning Thorfinn had come knocking at the hut's door, asking if they could go for a walk in the forest. Of course he'd not been interested in an actual walk, only in getting her in a secluded place so they could kiss and pleasure one another. Twice last month she had followed him into the woods, thinking it was time she found out what her body could offer but the experience had been far from conclusive. Twice his caresses had failed to do more than heat her blood and leave her frustrated. Now that she had felt what a man could do, how much pleasure she could have under his touch, the prospect of a clumsy fumble that would leave her unsatisfied had lost its appeal, as had Thorfinn.

He was attractive enough, tall and broad, with a charming smile, but his arrogance grated. She had barely been back a day and already he'd pounced on her in search for sexual gratification. He'd not even asked her how she was, even though he knew she'd been to war. The message was clear. He was not interested in her, only in what her hands could do.

Well, he had hands too, did he not? If he wanted release, he was going to have to use them, she was not going to do that for him ever again. They were done.

She forced herself to focus her attention back on Bragi, who was nodding toward her cropped hair. "You tried to go to battle like a man, didn't you, little girl?"

She bristled. After the frosty welcome she'd had from the people she loved the day before, she was not in the mood to endure teasing for people she despised.

"I didn't *try*. I did go. I fought and we won."

In the corner of her eye she saw Moon walking toward them. He would have seen her alone with Bragi and his friends and thought be had better come and help. They had not talked since he had called her the biggest mistake in his life but apparently, he would still come to her aid if need be. She could not help being grateful because she wasn't sure how she was going to rid herself of such brawny bullies.

Bragi gave a scoff, not in the least impressed by her reply. "A battle is no place for a woman. The only thing they're good for is a fuck after a good fight because there's nothing like it to rouse a man's blood."

No. Apparently not, she knew that from Farmon. And there was nothing like such comments to rouse her anger.

"They can only do that for men who know how to fight and go to actual battles, though, can't they," Eyja spat, "not for the ones who choose to stay at home with both their feet in the same shoe while the country is in danger."

"Hush, Imp!" Moon warned between his teeth as he drew near the group.

He had a point. Bragi would not like to be called a coward at the best of times, much less in front of his friends. But she was too incensed to care. He already thought her incapable of holding her tongue, so she might as well prove him right. It was time someone stood up to Bragi.

The tall man grabbed her by the chin, forcing her to look at him. Already knowing he would only get her again even if she managed to disentangle herself from his hold, Eyja met his gaze steadily and waited. There was little chance he would actually hurt her here, in the middle of the village, in full view of everyone, with Moon standing near, so she did not tremble.

"Take your hands off her."

She barely recognized Moon's voice, so icy had it gone and, though the warning was not aimed at her, she shivered.

Bragi ignored him and glared at her. "Hear me out. The only time a woman should open her mouth is to suck my c—"

"I *told* you to take your hands off her." Without further warning Moon pounced, hitting the awful man square in the jaw and sending him crashing to the ground.

The two other men fell on him in a flurry of limbs.

"No!"

Unable to help him in any way, Eyja ran to get Torsten, who was sharpening his axe outside his hut. Angry or not, he would not let his best friend or indeed anyone face three men on his own.

"Eyja? What's the ma—"

"Quick. I need your help. Now." After a brief hesitation, she gestured at his axe. "Take this as well." With luck, just seeing him appear armed with such a weapon would be enough to bring Bragi's friends to heel.

But that was not to be. By the time she'd managed to drag her brother to the well, a general fight had broken out. Apparently the young men in the village didn't need much incentive to let out some steam. They had no idea who had started the fight or why, yet they were all only too glad to join in. What had started as an altercation between three men for a good reason had turned into chaos.

Eyja wrung her hands, appalled. How was she going to put a stop to this? She could not just stand there while so many people ripped each other to shreds because of her, but what could she do? Torsten stared at the scene and then at her with wide eyes, as if to say he had no idea whose side he was supposed to take and what she expected him to do. And she had no idea what to tell him.

Someone fell to the ground at her feet, unconscious.

She screamed. "Stop, you morons!"

It was then that her father appeared. "What is going on here?"

When they heard him, the men instantly ceased fighting, such was the respect he commanded. They all straightened up and scattered without a word, all save the ones who had still not come to, and Moon, who stood his ground. He appeared relatively unscathed, even if his clothes were in disarray and his bottom lip was bleeding. Relieved beyond belief to see he had not been hurt, Eyja wanted to go and wipe the blood from his chin. He had fought for her, come to her defense unprompted, and even if the whole thing had descended into mayhem, the intention warmed her. He stared at her and shook his head slightly, as if to indicate they had better not give her father further cause for ire, so she stayed where she was.

Then he turned and walked away.

Torsten left as well, leaving her alone with her father, who crossed his arms over his chest. "Care to explain what happened, daughter?"

It was clear he had no doubt she was responsible for the chaos, which felt rather harsh. After all, no one had forced Bragi to talk to her with such venom or touch her like he would cattle, and the other men should have minded their own business. She had nothing to blame herself for.

"I'm sorry... But Bragi said those horrid things to me earlier. Moon was only—"

"Him, again! It seems that the two of you can only cause trouble when you're together."

Everything within her flared at that. If he thought it such a bad idea for them to be in contact, then why did he want to see them married? "And yet you'd have us bound for life!" she could not help but reply, letting her tongue run away with her once more.

The look he threw her froze the marrow in her bones. One year, when she was thirteen summers, their father had taken the whole family to his native Iceland for a few months. There they had discovered a wild, eerie land covered with huge sheets of pure blue ice called glaciers. Her father's eyes were this moment just as cold as the frozen landscape had been then.

Remote.

"I would have you bound to a man you chose to lie with if you are with child as a consequence of your actions. If you now think him a bad choice, then I cannot carry the blame for it."

So he still didn't believe her. "I told you we never—"

"And I wish I could believe you. But it is clear to me that there is something between you and Halfdan, something you're hiding, and I would have hoped you'd be honest about it. I expected more from you."

Pain sliced through her. She could handle his anger, his unfair accusations, but not his disappointment in her.

"I'm sorry I do not make you more proud, *Faðir*," she said on a sob, "but I'm trying my best. Apparently it's not enough. I'm sorry."

She ran away before he could answer, not certain she would like to hear what he had to say.

An oddity, a thief, a mistake, that was what she was for the people in the village. It was bad enough.

But now, to her own father, she was a liar and a disappointment.

FOR A WHOLE WEEK Eyja did little more than sleep, eat and work on a new set of clothes for Ari. Her mother had insisted she could help but she had refused the offer. It was her responsibility to replace the clothes she had borrowed and then ruined. Staying inside the hut had the added advantage of allowing her to avoid Moon. Hearing that he thought her the biggest mistake of his life had been more than she could bear. She had no intention of hearing what else he thought of her. And she didn't want to see anyone else, at the risk of provoking another disaster, of being accused of some horrid deed, or anything else that would make her father look at her with disapproval again, now that the peace was restored between them.

To her surprise, the evening after the incident with Bragi, he had sought her out to tell her she was not a disappointment to him, and he had never once in his life wished she were any different.

"You would not wish me to be less outspoken?" she had not been able to stop herself from asking. "Less stubborn? Less confrontational? Less reckless? Less—"

"No. I would never want you to be 'less anything,' or a boy either." How had he guessed that she had often wondered if he would not have preferred to have another son instead of a girl, another strong warrior in his image? "You are my daughter, and perfect the way you are, Eyja. Just like your outspoken, stubborn, confrontational, reckless mother. Why do you think I fell in love with her? Strong men need strong women in their lives. I learned it the hard way. So I will not let you be anything else than your beautiful self."

"Oh, *Faðir!*"

She had cried and buried her face into his chest, relishing the knowledge that she was loved, no matter what.

Then one morning she woke up to a familiar and not altogether pleasant sensation. She was wet between the legs and there was a weight in her lower abdomen. Her flux had come. In other words, she finally had the means to prove to the whole village that she was not with child. After placing the protective pad in place, she spent a long moment lying in bed, unsure what to feel or how to announce it. Would her father even accept the proof that she had been telling the truth? Would he not believe she had fabricated false evidence just to get herself out of a union with Moon? After all, much as he loved her, he seemed to think her capable of the worst.

No, she was being silly. Of course he would believe her. The best way was to get this over with as quickly as possible.

She found her mother at the back of the hut, digging up weeds, getting the soil ready for winter. Her hair was streaked with silver now, and yet she was as beautiful as ever. Her father at least thought so, Eyja knew.

Only the night before she had overheard a tender conversation between them.

"You have never looked better, wife." There was a pause, during which Eyja assumed they exchanged a kiss. Her parents always kissed, even when they weren't alone. "You have silvery strands in your copper hair now and it struck me the other day that the only metal missing on you is gold. So I went to Caedmon, and asked him to make a chain of gold for you to wear."

Another silence, during which her father presumably handed over the chain—and possibly kissed her again. When her mother spoke, she did so with a shaky voice.

"It's beautiful. Oh, Wolf. I love you. I will never stop being thankful for the day you bought me at that auction."

Tears blurring her vision, Eyja had fled into the forest. Her parents had the perfect marriage, one built on love and respect. No one had forced them to marry, they had simply chosen one another. Well, that had happened after Wolf had bought Merewen from a slave trader, but that was beside the point. He had never intended to keep her as a slave but had definitely wanted her as a wife. And Sigurd and Frigyth, Moon's parents, were just as happily matched. And yet these men who had married the women of their choice would have forced their children into a union neither wanted. It didn't make sense.

"Eyja." Her mother placed the hoe against the fence and walked up to her with a smile. Around her neck was the gold chain she'd received the night before. It was exquisite, highlighting the copper sparks in her hair and making her eyes glow, just as her father had no doubt intended. "You look a bit pale. Are you all right?"

"Yes. I bled this morning," she told her in a flat voice, knowing she would understand the significance of the words immediately.

"I see. Come, let us go for a walk."

With those words her mother took her by the arm and led her toward the forest. They often took walks together, it was a good way to air out any concerns they might have or simply share a laugh together.

"So tell me. Are you relieved?"

"No." How could she be relieved or surprised, or anything else? She knew she would have her flux, sooner or later. There was no other way, as she had not slept with any man. "I know no one believes me but I always knew I would not be with child. I cannot be. I told you. Moon and I never actually lay together."

In the end she had not finished her confession the other day, and revealed what he had done to her. There had been no need. Her mother seemed to have understood what had happened well enough.

"I know. Virgins have no chance of carrying a babe."

Eyja stopped on her tracks. "So. You believe me?"

"Eyja. You are my daughter. Of course I believe you. If you tell me you're still untouched, then that's what you are. I trust you."

"I am *Faðir*'s daughter as well, and yet *he* doesn't believe me," she said dejectedly.

"Deep down, I'm sure he does."

Eyja could not help a snort. "If he does, he has an odd way of showing it."

"Tell me. Do you really think he would force you to marry a man you don't want? Think carefully, and be fair."

There was only one answer to that question. "No, he

wouldn't. But then I don't understand. Why would he insist on making Moon and I think we might have to marry if he means to leave that decision to me?"

"He will have his reasons." Her mother shook her head. "I cannot pretend to always know what goes on in the mighty wolf's head. All I know is that you can rely on his love and support, no matter what."

"Yes. I do know that."

They walked on, then her mother spoke again. "You know... Your father would never admit to it, but when we discovered you were missing, he took it hardest of all. He hated himself for not having been able to stop you from putting yourself in danger. He has spent the last thirty years protecting everyone from the village, making sure they're safe. For the first time he'd failed someone and it was you, his own daughter." A pause. "I'm afraid it brought back painful memories for him."

Yes. Eyja knew her father had been married to an Icelander before he'd met her mother. The poor woman had been killed by a greedy neighbor who had accused Wolf of the crime and forced him to go into exile. That was one of the reasons he had taken the role as leader of the village. He had wanted to atone for a murder he saw as his fault. He thought he should have been able to protect his first wife.

"He didn't fail me. I decided to go," she contradicted. "I wanted to go. I'm an adult now, I can make my own decisions."

Merewen sighed. "I know. But you're still his daughter, still the baby he held in his arms and kissed as soon as you were born. I think deep down you understand why he would feel this way, even if you resent it."

Yes, unfortunately she did. If she had children of her own one day, she would do everything to make sure they were all right, no matter how old they were.

"Come, let's go back home and tell your father there is no

child, as expected. He and Sigurd are meeting with a Saxon from town right now but he will want to know that you've bled as soon as they're finished."

As they exited the forest they met her brother Steinar, back from the river with a basket full of fish. Eyja stiffened, not knowing how he would react. Since she'd come back, things had been difficult with her brothers, Torsten in particular. They didn't seem to accept the fact that she'd been intimate with a man they considered as part of the family, which she could understand to a certain extent. It had unsettled her as well at first. But still, that did not give them the right to withdraw their affection from her. If she had managed to make her peace with it, they could certainly do the same. After all, it was none of their business what she did and who with, and perhaps now that she had been proven right, they would thaw toward her. She hoped so because they were very dear to her and she missed them.

"Are you all right, brother?" she asked.

"Yes, thank you. I was on my way to see *Faðir*."

That he was using this as an excuse to take his leave was obvious but, as that was precisely what she was doing as well, she did not let it bother her. "So were we, so we can all go together," she said, taking him by the arm. He stiffened but did not disentangle his arm, which she took as an encouraging sign. "Mother was telling me he's with Sigurd and a man from town. We'll go wait for him and—"

She stopped in her tracks when the door to the hut opened on the visiting Saxon. It was a man she knew only too well, one she had hoped never to see again.

Farmon.

All the blood iced in her veins, rooting her to the spot. What was he doing here? But, of course, as he lived in town, he would have guessed where to find two local Norsemen he wanted to take his revenge on. Their village was the only Norse settlement for miles around. As they had joined at the same time as he and his friends, it stood to reason that it was where he would find them.

She let go of her brother's arm and took refuge behind his massive body, knowing he would shield her from view most efficiently. Hopefully Farmon, who'd been deep in conversation with her father, hadn't seen her.

"Go tell Moon he needs to hide," she told Steinar, panic threatening to overwhelm her.

"Hide?"

"No time to explain. Find him, now, tell him to join me in the forest." She spoke barely above a whisper, her speech altered by fear. "Tell him Farmon is here. He'll understand. Make sure he hides his face while he's in the village. Go! Please."

With those words, she ran away as fast as her legs could carry her.

What was Farmon doing here? Had he come to make them pay for leaving without warning and making a fool of him? Or to finally put his threat to execution and have her service him and his whole pack of men like a whore, no matter what she said?

Well, this time she and Moon weren't alone. The villagers would defend them if necessary, her father would eat Farmon alive and spit out his bones before he'd had time to understand what had hit him. She had nothing to fear, she was safe here.

Despite this assurance, when she finally reached the cover of the trees, she fell to her knees.

CHAPTER TWELVE

W hat now?

Moon had been surprised to see Steinar come to him earlier. It was obvious Eyja's brother was reluctant to deliver his sister's message and, in truth, he wasn't sure he wanted to go see her. Was it a trap? Would he not find himself involved in another mess of her making? Nothing was guaranteed with her and he would prefer to stay well clear of it this time. Nevertheless, as soon as Farmon's name had been mentioned, Moon had known he had no choice but to go and see her. Steinar didn't know the man, had no idea why he would pose danger to either of them, so he could not have made the threat up and Eyja would never use such an appalling trick as to lie about a man wanting to rape her to lure him in.

No, it had to be true. The Saxon really was in the village, looking for them. If that was the case, she did need his protection. He could not leave her on her own with such a bastard roaming around. Using his hood to cover his face as he'd been instructed, he hurried toward the woods.

He found Eyja in the clearing, exactly in the place he had imagined she would be, by the gnarled oak. She was staring at the ground, her face white as milk, her body heaving. It was clear that she had just been sick.

Oh no. He could think of only one thing that made otherwise healthy women sick.

"Are you…" Bile rose in his own throat and he couldn't finish the sentence. But she couldn't be with child, could she? Not when he had not entered her body or come anywhere near her. He'd made sure not to soil her with his seed, so how could she be pregnant?

"It's n-nothing," she stammered. "I'm fine."

"You're not fine," he snapped back. "You've just been sick. People who are fine do not cast the contents of their stomach onto the ground. Are you with child?" This time he forced himself to ask the question. He had to know.

"No."

Everything within him melted in relief because for a dreadful moment he'd wondered if she was not carrying someone else's child. She had not allowed Thorfinn to sleep with her and she'd been a virgin that day in the forest but she might have allowed another man to take her to bed since their return to the village. But that had been less than two weeks ago. Could she suffer from nausea after so short a time?

No, he was being silly and she had just told him that, thankfully, she was not with child. He exhaled. Then worry spiked through him again. Pregnant or not, she had just been sick. It was not normal.

"Are you unwell?" Steinar had not mentioned his sister was not well earlier. "What ails you?"

Instead of answering, Eyja shook her head. Moon frowned. There had to be something, and there was only one other thing that could explain the bout of sickness.

Fear.

Fear sometimes made people lose control over their bodies

and he knew that Farmon was here in the village. It was not hard to guess that the man must be responsible for her anguish. But why? Surely she knew she didn't have anything to fear here in the village? Everyone would defend her, the bloody Saxon would not be allowed to touch as much as her little finger. So... He hesitated to form the thought. Was she afraid because she remembered something that had happened instead of worrying about what *could* happen?

He took another step toward her. "What happened with Farmon? How did he find out you were a woman, exactly? You never told me."

And suddenly it seemed vital that he knew. Had the Saxon actually raped her? Was that why she'd wanted to leave the company of men?

She hesitated and hugged herself for far too long. Finally, she spoke.

"The morning we went into the woods together... He saw us."

Moon felt as if he wanted to retch himself. The man had seen them, perhaps even watched them. The idea that the bastard had witnessed Eyja's most intimate moment, seen him give her pleasure and then bring himself to climax was horrifying.

He'd thought the men had heard her moans and that had been bad enough. This was a hundred times worse.

Eyja started talking again, her voice flat. "He said... He said all those horrible things, how he would like to use me and then let his men take their well-earned pleasure with me. He pressed me against the tree when I tried to flee."

He stilled. Of course. The bruised cheek. He'd known she hadn't walked into a tree! He should have insisted, forced her to reveal the truth.

This was all his fault. Why, oh, why had he left her alone in such a vulnerable moment? She'd been bewildered by what he'd done to her, he should have stayed with her, made sure she was all right. Although Moon wasn't sure he would be able to endure hearing the rest, he had to ask.

"Did he touch you?" Had she had time to get dressed before Farmon pounced on her? This was his worst nightmare come true, being forced to admit that a woman's rape was all his fault, even if he had not been the one to perpetrate the crime.

"No. One of the men called him just then. He left, saying he would reveal the truth about my identity to his friends during the day, and that I had better get ready for a rough night." She started to shiver. "If we hadn't left when the boars attacked, that night they would have each taken a turn with me."

Yes, this much Moon already knew. But he'd had no idea she had borne that burden alone the whole day. He slapped the nearest tree so hard pain reverberated all the way to his ribs.

"Damn it, Eyja, why didn't you tell me Farmon knew the truth? You should have—"

"And then what? I would have had to watch you being ripped to shreds by eight men for defending me." She stood up, still pale but as determined as ever. "You would have died in front of my eyes, and then they would have raped me anyway. Your death would have been in vain. The only solution was to leave."

She was right, damn her! If she had told him, he would only have gotten killed for attacking the men on his own, and his death would have made no difference to the fate they had in store for her. Still, he couldn't help feeling she should have come to him.

"The bastard!" he said between his teeth. Farmon was lucky. If Moon had known how the Saxon had threatened and frightened her before, he would have gone to rip his guts out instead of hiding and coming to see Eyja as she'd instructed. "He had better make sure he and I never cross paths again."

But even as the words passed his lips he realized he might well ensure their paths did cross again. If Farmon had been able to track them down to the village, Moon could certainly do the same and scour the town in search of him. It might take time but he would eventually find him and avenge Eyja.

Just then, as if fate had decided to save him some time, he saw a man walking in the distance, on the road leading back to town. It was none other than Farmon. Moon didn't even blink. With a roar, he started to run.

"No, Moon! Wait, we're supposed to hide," he heard Eyja shout before she chased after him. But he wouldn't hide. Not when he had to make the bastard pay for what he'd done. Today Farmon was not surrounded by his cronies, he was on his own—and he would pay.

He fell on the unsuspecting Saxon and pinned him against the nearest tree. Fury was blinding his vision, urging him to throttle the man on the spot. When Eyja drew next to him, begging him to let go, he barely heard her.

"Please, don't hurt me!" the man wheezed. "Have mercy."

The plea only incensed Moon further. Why should he even listen to the maggot? "You dare talk to me of mercy when you—"

He froze in the act of strangling Farmon because... Well, because the man he was holding wasn't Farmon. It couldn't be. Despite what he'd been told, and what he'd thought at first, he could not ignore the evidence in front of his eyes.

"You don't have any scars on your cheek," he whispered, slackening his hold. This was indisputable proof that he was not the man who'd fought with them in York. A scar could appear on someone's cheek but not suddenly disappear, especially not one so fresh or dramatic.

"Why w-would I have a s-scar?" the man stammered, clearly at a loss, and frightened for his life.

"You're not Farmon," Moon repeated, doing his best to clear the red haze from his mind. He needed to let go. This was not the man he was after, but an innocent. Still, he found it hard to relinquish his hold over him.

"No, I'm not Farmon." This time the Saxon sounded more assured, as if he trusted that he had nothing to fear now that his real identity had been revealed. Moon was not so confident. In spite of knowing he would feel bad afterward for throttling the wrong man, he was having a hard time mastering his fury. "Who are you? What do you want with Farmon?"

The question brought some sense back into him and Moon finally found the strength to release the man. He glared at him while he cleared his throat. Though he now knew this was not his worst enemy, it was hard to recover from the towering rage that had consumed him only moments ago. Besides, the man looked too much like Farmon for him to relax completely. What was going on here? The two of them had to be related.

"You answer my questions first. Who are you? And how do you know who I'm talking about?"

"I'm Cuthbert, his twin brother. You're not the first one to mistake me for him, as you can imagine. Although usually people don't try to throttle me when they do. I wouldn't be surprised if that was what they wanted to do but, as a rule, they lack the guts to try."

Considering he had almost been killed a moment ago, the man demonstrated impressive calm. In fact, his whole demeanor was different Farmon's. There was none of the loathsome swagger and crudeness his twin displayed. He was soft-spoken and seemed genuinely sorry for the confusion, even if he had been the one suffering from it. It was only because he'd glimpsed him from a distance that Moon had been fooled. Had he spent but a moment with him he would have known this could not be Farmon.

"I gather that you know him?" the Saxon continued.

Know him. Yes, unfortunately he did.

"We marched with him to go fight the Norsemen," Moon answered curtly. That was all the man needed to know. The rest was none of his business.

"I'd heard that he and some of his friends had joined the king's men." A pause. "I take it he survived the battle, if you mistook me for him?"

"Yes."

"Well. My parents will be glad of it at least," Cuthbert said with a nod. It was obvious that he didn't share the same relief but Moon didn't ask any questions. If the man didn't get on with his brother, it went to show that he knew him for the weasel he was. Yet another reason to regret the misguided assault. He took another step back, indicating the Saxon was safe.

"Forgive me. I didn't mean to hurt you."

"No, I can see that. And I'm sorry for whatever reason pushed you to do it."

It was brief but Moon didn't miss the way Cuthbert glanced in Eyja's direction. It was as if he'd guessed why a man might want to strangle his brother. Evidently Farmon was used to assaulting the women he met and this was not the first occurrence.

"Can I ask you a favor? I won't hold it against you if you refuse, but I have to at least try. You seem like a man of honor."

The Saxon shuffled on his feet. "Of course."

"I take it from your questions that Farmon has not come back home yet." A brief nod confirmed this. "Would you send word to the village when he does? I would be very grateful." He forced himself to be honest, even if he knew it might not help his cause. "I feel compelled to tell you that I cannot vouch for my reaction if I ever cross paths with your brother but in the meantime, I..."

"You want to know whether you can relax your guard or not," Cuthbert finished in his stead. "You want to know that, for now at least, you can live your life without worrying when my brother might pounce."

"Yes." That was exactly what it was, only he would not have dared admit as much to Farmon's brother, who was not responsible for the man's character.

"I understand. You want to protect your wife. It's only normal."

"She's..." Moon started with the intention of saying that Eyja was not his wife but his mouth had other ideas. "She's very precious to me."

He started. Where had that come from? Oh, well, it was the truth at least. The imp *was* precious to him, even if she wasn't his wife, and he didn't want her harmed. He stole a brief glance at her and saw that she was still too pale for comfort. Before he could think, he drew her against his flank.

"I promise I will let you know when he comes back," Cuthbert said. "But don't be surprised if you have to wait. It might be weeks, or even months before he does. I know he was considering leaving town."

Even better. The longer the bastard decided to stay away, the better.

"I'm Halfdan. Send word directly to me, please." He would not have Eyja dealing with the message on her own. Besides, he wouldn't put it past her to hide the news so as to spare him if she heard that Farmon was back.

After a last nod, the Saxon walked away.

Moon turned around slowly. Eyja was standing next to him, looking smaller than usual. It struck him that he was surprised to see her wear a dress when in reality there was nothing more normal than this. He rubbed the back of his neck, unsure what to do or what to say. Since they had come back to the village, everything had gone awry. They had been berated for their decision to join the army, they had argued, he had found himself involved in a fight with a bully talking to her as he would to a whore and then they had spent more than a week without seeing one another, the longer they had ever done.

It had hit him unexpectedly hard.

As a youth, he'd often complained about the fact that she was always around, even when he didn't want her to be, but he now realized how helpful and comforting her presence had been. As a woman, she'd brought a much welcome breath of fresh air and a new angle to the proceedings. Left to their own devices, a group of boys could all too easily have become feral and obnoxious, like Bragi and Farmon's little packs had done. Eyja had brought some sense and restraint to the whole affair.

And joy.

Having taken for granted the fact that he saw her every day, he'd been surprised by how much he'd missed her these last few days. Perhaps he should not have been, for the imp was one of a kind. No one he knew could have taken her place, for no one was more sharp-minded, or more stimulating. He needed that constant stimulation, so he just wanted things to go back to the way they'd been. Or at least... to something. Being without her was just too odd. He felt incomplete, somehow.

"Listen, Imp, I'm sorry for what I said the other day, for saying that I regretted what happened between us, for shouting at you, for telling you that you were a mistake. None of that is true. I don't regret anything and I wish I had not snapped thus."

By the gods, it seemed he was forever apologizing to her for losing patience and hurting her feelings.

"And I'm sorry for how badly I handled the situation with my father," she mumbled, not looking at him, "for allowing him to believe we had lain together, for provoking Bragi and causing him and his friends to—"

"Don't be sorry. He had it coming. I will not have him or anyone else treat you the way he did. I hope you know I will always be on your side."

"I know. You've just proved it and I thank you."

He cupped her jaw in his hands. He'd meant the gesture as a reassurance, but it ended up looking rather possessive, if not predatory. He was instantly reminded of Thorfinn, who might have cupped her face thus before he'd kissed her. Could he do the same, draw her closer to him and place his lips against hers? They'd been intimate once, very intimate, but they had never kissed, and suddenly it seemed like something he wanted to remedy.

No.

He took a step back and forced himself to release her. He could not do something as irresponsible. Things were complicated enough as they were. In any case, he should not want to kiss her, and now least of all, when they had just found out that they would not be forced to marry. Not that he'd had any doubt about it, of course. What they had done could never have led to a pregnancy.

"So you're not with child then," he said slowly. "Our fathers will have no choice but to accept that you are still a virgin and we won't have to marry."

"No, we won't."

Eyja sounded as breathless as he was. There was an odd expression on her face, one he could not quite account for. Was she... disappointed? Was *he*? Was that what the odd churning in his gut was?

Surely not.

They stared at one another for a long moment, and he had the sudden certainty that everything would be all right from now on. She would not avoid him any longer. Relief swept though him. They would be friends again, she would be part of his life once more.

"Will you come with me to tell *Faðir* we were telling the truth all along?"

Moon nodded and held out his hand to her. "Of course. Let's go."

So it was all over.

Eyja stared at the beams overhead, wondering what was causing her despondency. Shouldn't she be relieved she wouldn't have to spend the rest of her life married to a man she had not chosen? A man who felt for her none of the things her father felt for her mother, a man who didn't want her for his wife? Yes, she should. And she was relieved, in a way. It was only...

Well, that in another, she wasn't.

This talk of being married to Moon seemed to have put strange ideas and hopes into her head and she could not help but think of what might have been if they had been forced to marry. Would it have been so terrible to be his wife, even if they had not loved one another? After all, her parents, whose marriage was the kind she was striving for, had not married *because* they were in love. But love had quickly followed.

Perhaps it could have been the same for her and Moon? They already knew and liked each other. She made him laugh and he made her feel safe. She could think of worse circumstances to start a marriage. And, of course, there was the knowledge of what fire he could ignite in her body when they touched...

Unable to sleep despite the late hour, she slipped outside. Sitting on the bench her father had made the year she was born, she raised her eyes to the moon, which was casting its light above the land, turning everything blue. There it was, in the middle of the sky like a faithful friend, drawn by Máni's chariot. It was a familiar, comforting presence and yet ever changing. Tonight it was full and round, in a few days time it would be reduced to a mere crescent and then gone completely, only to grow again—and wane again the following month. Immovable and yet always different. Even the color could change. It sometimes abandoned its usual silver to turn white, blood red or even amber.

And Moon...

Why could it not be the same with him? Why could he not assume different roles in her life? In just a few weeks, he had gone from brother, playing companion, friend and protector to lover. He'd made her discover pleasure and he could have ended up as her husband. The moon, that nightly body, was sometimes visible during the day, when you least expected it. Why couldn't it be the same with her Moon? Why couldn't he be where she'd least expected to find him?

Or... Was it so unexpected?

It was far from certain.

Aged fifteen, when the workings of her mind had started to change along with her body, she had been briefly attracted to each of her male friends in turn. For the most part, the feelings had vanished as suddenly as they had appeared, never to come back. But with Moon... With Moon it had been different, stronger, more lasting, to the point that she had once carved in an old oak a shape, the exact replica of the mark on his wrist. She had not just been drawn to his physique, she had once fancied herself in love with him, which was not quite the same.

Well, it just went to show how foolish she was.

Because he certainly did not feel anything more than affection toward her.

CHAPTER THIRTEEN

"**I**s it true that you almost wed Eyja?"

Moon lifted his head from the basket he was weaving and arched a brow. His cousin Rorik had appeared out of nowhere and was leaning against the side of the hut, a smile floating on his lips. Something about that smile caused Moon's heart to start beating faster in his chest. What did the man know that he didn't?

"Why do you ask?"

He'd assumed no one knew about what had been decided by Wolf and his father with regards to him and Eyja. Had he been wrong? Did the whole village know? The idea sat ill with him.

"I heard your mother tell mine today," Rorik explained. Ah, that made sense, the two sisters shared everything. It was only a question of time before Dunne was told about the proposed match. "I could scarce believe my ears."

"Why?" For a reason he could not fathom, the idea that someone who knew him and Eyja could not believe in a union between them displeased him. Surely there would be worse matches?

A shrug answered him. "I don't know. I suppose I've so

often heard you complain about her being where you didn't want her to be that I never thought you would bear to see even more of her. It would be like me saying I'm considering marrying Liv."

Yes. Everyone knew Rorik and the carpenter's daughter didn't get on. Which was why it was not the same thing at all. He and Eyja not only got on well, they liked and respected each other. They could easily have found contentment as husband and wife. Instead of pointing it out, Moon resumed the weaving of the basket.

"In any case, what would it be to you if we married and I was unhappy?" he couldn't help but ask.

But... Would he really be unhappy married to Eyja, he wondered? He was not so sure.

Rorik's smile widened. "Oh, what you two do is nothing to me. But I bet you didn't know I have kissed her."

The twig in Moon's hand snapped and he almost let out a curse. Thorfinn, now his own cousin... Would the whole male population come to him to reveal they had once kissed the brazen imp? To think he had taken her for an innocent! Virgin she might be, but she was clearly not untouched. Well, he should have known.

"When did that happen?" he asked, doing his best to sound uninterested. He was not entirely sure he succeeded but he had to know.

"The day she turned seventeen, she asked me to kiss her. I agreed. She looked so adorable with all those flowers in her hair, I could not resist."

As it happened, Moon remembered very well the way she had looked that day, and "those flowers" had been gathered and woven into her hair by none other than his own sisters. It had been their present for her special day. They had worked all morning to get her ready. He remembered his surprise when he had seen her emerge from the hut looking clean and feminine for once, in a long white dress and elaborate hairstyle. Not that she was dirty or masculine exactly, but thus far he had only ever seen her with her hair loose and in a serviceable, plain dress. More often than not, the long tresses had been tangled and the dress had borne traces of her recent run through the woods.

That day he had seen for the first time that she was different from her burly brothers, and not a child anymore, but a young woman. The flowers in her hair had made him see her for the beauty she had become.

If he had known they had served to attract that wretched Rorik, he would have crushed them to dust before they could go anywhere near her head.

"Well, we both know she's always been after thrills. Don't feel too special. It didn't mean anything. The following day she probably asked your brother Ralph to bury her up to her neck in mud, just to see how it felt like. Or are you telling me you did more than kiss her?" he added with narrowed eyes.

Fortunately for his sanity, Rorik laughed. Ah. So he had not. "No. We kissed a few times but we both knew it would never lead anywhere. It is as you say, she was only after a first kiss from a handsome man skilled in the art of seduction and, as I happen to fit the description, she chose me."

Relief mingled with irritation swept through Moon. The arrogant bastard was too good looking for his own good. Fortunately, he was also too personable for anyone to take exception to him.

"Be off with you," he grunted. "I'm sure there are plenty of females hankering after kisses around here. You shouldn't keep them waiting."

"There are. Never fear, I shall find them."

Once Rorik had gone, Moon put the basket to one side. Finishing it would have to wait. He would only break all his twigs if he carried on, and create a poor product. His father, who had taught him the skill, would not be impressed if he handed him a creel that would let fish through like a sieve. Right now he was incapable of focusing on the task. He just wanted to see Eyja. The day before they had made peace and he wanted to make the most of it.

He found her by the geese pen, feeding the animals. She was talking to them as she threw the seeds, asking all sorts of questions they had no hope of answering before allowing them their portion of food. Amused, he watched her a moment. Did she ever do things the way they were supposed to be done? Whoever demanded that their geese performed some trick to earn their food?

"I'm curious. What happens if they cannot tell you how many eggs they have laid so far this month?" he asked, causing her to jump. "Do you let them starve?"

"Moon." She turned to face him. "You made me jump."

"I saw. That's what comes of being too focused on honking animals."

She smiled at him. He stilled, stunned by the beauty of this smile. Had she always smiled thus? If she had, he had never reacted to it thus.

He cleared his throat while she threw the last of the seed without asking anything. The geese, no doubt relieved to be fed without having to prove themselves first, ran to the pile.

"Was there anything you wanted?" Eyja asked, shaking her apron free of dust.

Yes, as a matter of fact there was. He was about to ask her about Rorik, Thorfinn, and demand to know just how many men she had kissed, when he spotted Sigrid walking out of the forge. Earlier that year he had shared a few wild nights with Bee's widowed friend. That summer it had been a woman in town. It suddenly occurred to him that he would hate if Eyja asked him how many women he had been intimate with, as she was sure to, because the number would be uncomfortably high. And he had done a lot more than just kiss them.

Better to come back to his senses and let her lead the conversation. One of the things he loved about her was that he could never quite predict the direction her mind would take. They could be talking about her brothers and she would suddenly wonder if the baby tits in the oak by the village hall had left their nest yet. It made for fascinating, if disjointed conversations.

As if to prove they had better follow her lead, she asked, quite out of the blue, "Do you remember the time I came back home with a black eye?"

A smile tugged at his lips and he didn't try to fight it. "Which time?"

Eyja swatted Moon on the arm at the cheeky question. The wretched man! His grin was far too wide, he was enjoying himself far too much remembering just how wild she had been as a child for her to allow the comment to pass unnoticed.

"Silly!" She should have known he would tease her.

"I'm not being silly. You were as reckless as any boy and got yourself in all sorts of scrapes. You still do."

There was no point arguing the point. She did. Hadn't she proved it by going to war? Besides, he didn't seem to mind. He'd even made it sound like a compliment, and Eyja preferred to be praised for her spirit rather than the color of her eyes, or anything else she had no control over. It was much more meaningful to be appreciated for one's achievements than for one's physique. Her appearance was something she owed to her parents, not to her own merit. Thorfinn had complimented her curves, enthused about the pertness of her breasts, no doubt thinking she would be pleased. She had not. After all, if he had thought her scrawny and her breasts sagging, she would have been unable to do anything about it. But with a different shape to her hips or a fuller bosom, she would still be the same intrepid imp Moon appreciated. It was what mattered.

Rather than finding her lacking, he admired her for what many people might have found off-putting.

"Anyway. The reason I was hurt was, that day I'd been practicing with a sling. Yours," she added, feeling herself redden. Why was she confiding this now? She had no idea. Perhaps because after having had to endure his absence for days, she relished his presence. People who had food at their disposal without having to hunt or forage for it never knew what hunger was. Then the day they had to go without, it was a shock. The depravation hit them all the harder.

It had been the same with her and Moon. He'd always been a part of her life and she'd never questioned the fact that they saw each other every day, or very nearly. And then suddenly she'd had to go a whole week without exchanging a single word with him. It had been hard to deal with.

Now they were talking again and she wanted to make the most it.

Except... except she had angered him.

Again.

"You! You were the one who stole my sling?" he roared. "I *knew* I hadn't lost it! Damn it, Imp, it took me days to make another one! And then I had to adapt my technique as it was not as pliable and soft as the first one had been."

"I'm sorry, I had intended to return it, of course, but I broke it during my experiments and I never found the courage to tell you." She bit her bottom lip, feeling ridiculous. *Why* did she have to mention this? They had only just started to talk again, now was not the time to infuriate him anew. That damn tongue of hers. Her inability to hold it seemed to get worse by the day. "Anyway, I guess what I'm trying to say is that I've always wanted to know how to use a sling. You made it look so easy, so satisfying."

There was a silence. Was he about to storm away? No, to her surprise, he sighed and brushed the corner of her left eye, where the stone had hit her all those years ago. So he remembered which side had been bruised. She was stupidly moved.

"I could show you how to use a sling if you wanted. It would save you from injuring yourself the next time you try to do it on your own. Better that than having to make yet another sling when you help yourself to mine."

Eyja's whole body sagged in relief. He wasn't mad. He was even teasing her.

Then excitement shot through her veins at the prospect of finally being able to use the deadly instrument. Moon probably had no idea, but she had spent many hours watching him practice the skill by the river. There was something intensely satisfying in seeing objects topple over or explode when you hadn't even seen the stone fly in the air toward it. It was almost supernatural.

"Could we start now?"

He laughed. "Trust you to be so impatient, Imp! No, not now. Eirik is waiting for me, I agreed to go into town with him this afternoon." She forced herself not to let her disappointment show. The twinkle in Moon's eye told her she did not quite succeed. He leaned in toward her. "But tomorrow perhaps?"

The promise of spending a day together with Moon, just like in the old days, was irresistible. A wide grin split her mouth.

"Yes, tomorrow. Meet me at the well shortly after dawn with your sling. I know the perfect place."

"Do you intend to lead me all the way back to York? I should have guessed you had an evil design in mind."

Moon was surprised. Eyja had taken him a lot farther from the village than he had expected. They could have practiced with the sling pretty much anywhere but she had elected to take him to a part of the forest they rarely explored as it was a lot wilder than the ones surrounding the village. What on earth did she have in mind?

"Of course not, silly. Have patience," she answered, not even glancing his way. He could not help a snort. *She* was exhorting *him* to patience? Really, the imp had some gall.

He followed her, admiring the way she navigated between bushes and avoided rocks without ever faltering or slowing down. She was as nimble and sure-footed as a goat. She was also, now that he thought of it, as independent and stubborn as one. What would she do if he told her she reminded him of the animal? Probably charge at him—just like a wild goat. He smiled to himself. Better to keep quiet.

After a while she came to a halt. It was obvious she knew why she had chosen this place, even if it looked rather unremarkable to him.

"Do you remember the time I came back home with bleeding knuckles?" she asked, throwing him a sideways glance.

Moon recognized a challenge when he saw one and he raised to it without hesitation.

"Which time?" Judging from her grin, that was just the answer she'd been hoping for. This renewed companionship between them was enjoyable, he had to admit. It was like it had been before, only... different. Like the subtle difference between sunset and sunrise. Similar and yet not quite the same.

"When I was about sixteen," she specified. "Well, this is why my hand was damaged, because I carved this."

She nodded to the oak behind him. Moon peered at it and

saw a pale shape in the bark, level with his chest. Time had blurred its edges somewhat but it was still recognizable as a moon. It was exactly the same shape as the mark on his wrist. He brushed his finger along it wonderingly.

"Why did you do that?"

She shrugged, as if she wasn't sure herself. "I was infatuated with you at the time, and I'd just seen you kiss another girl. Instead of slashing at her, I stormed out of the village and took my frustration out on the poor tree. I guess I wanted to carve into something the memory of the feelings I had for you. Silly, I know, but that's what it was."

He stilled, as stunned as if she had just used his sling to send a stone to his temple and hit her mark. "You... were infatuated with me?"

This was new information, information he was not sure what to make of.

"Don't feel special," the imp had the audacity to answer, the exact words he had told Rorik only the day before. "At that time I was infatuated with nearly all the men close to me in age. You know I was always reckless and in search of new experiences."

Yes, he did know. Again, this was exactly what he had told Rorik. She had always been after thrills, that was why she had asked his cousin to kiss her aged seventeen, no other reason! He'd been right. Relief washed through him.

"And just how many of these men did you actually kiss?" he asked, doing his best to appear calm when the idea of her in another man's arms set his blood to boil.

"A few. I had to get familiar with how it works, you understand." Her answer, along with the glance she threw him, was mischief personified.

"Was Rorik one of them?" Surely the man hadn't lied?

She made a dismissive gesture of the hand. "Oh, that one was years ago. It hardly counts."

"And Thorfinn?" The man had been quite clear, their tryst had happened very recently and they had done a lot more than kissing.

This time she blinked. "How do you even—"

"Never mind how. Answer me."

"No." The contrary minx crossed her arms and planted herself in front of him. "You answer me first. How do you know about him and me?"

Moon forced himself not to let his admiration show. With her eyes ablaze, her chin lifted and her proud stance, she was magnificent, every inch the indomitable warrior she had tried to be in the army, even if she barely reached to his shoulder. He briefly wondered if he would be attracted to a woman who did not display such beguiling self-confidence in the future. Suddenly a fiery nature seemed to be the only thing guaranteed to catch his attention. This was a problem, because there were not many who could match the imp in sheer brazenness. But after having known her, he feared that any other attitude would fail to rouse his interest, perhaps even his blood. The thought made him shiver. What would he do if he stopped feeling desire? He was only twenty-eight, damn it all, he could not lead a chaste life!

Pushing thoughts of elusive future conquests—or lack thereof—out of his mind, he answered Eyja's question.

"Thorfinn told me you'd been seeing him before we left." She blanched, as well she might. The man had no business going around discussing her private life with other people. "He said that you'd given each other pleasure. Or at least, that *you* gave *him* pleasure. I'm not sure he reciprocated the favor."

"He did not."

The way she lowered her eyes sent blood shooting straight to his groin. Moon knew with absolute certainty she was thinking of the way he had licked her in that forest and made her explode in release. His mouth started to water at the memory. They had better change the subject before he tumbled her to the ground and did it again, this time unhampered by braies. Perhaps talking about her and the men she'd had in her arms was not the best idea.

There was one last question he needed to ask, however. "Were you ever interested in my brothers?"

"Well." She looked at him again and made a grimace. "Elwyn was already married to Bee by then, so, of course, he was not one of the men I considered. But Eirik, now, that's different. He's rather..."

The imp let the words hang, as if to tease him. Moon clenched his jaw, because it worked, damn it all. The idea of her lusting after all the boys in the village, his own brother included, was not one to please him. And what was Eirik, exactly, except a big oaf?

"What did you carve for him, I wonder? He doesn't have any marks on his body, at least not that *I* can see. But perhaps you had access to parts of him I would shudder to see, so we will never know."

"No, we'll never know, because I never had access to those parts either."

When she let out a pearly laugh, he made a show of looking at the forest around him. "Did you find enough trees here to record all your conquests?"

She shook her head slowly when he had expected her to laugh again. "You were the only one I carved something for, Moon."

His heart tripped in his chest at the confession and the throaty way she'd said his name. Now *that* had to mean something, as had the fact that she'd decided to admit it to him so easily. But what?

She stared at him, and all the air was sucked out of his lungs.

The bewildering impulse to kiss her seized him again. He knew why he'd wanted to do it when he'd handed her into the barrel on the river Dent. They had been about to be separated and in mortal danger, so it was understandable. He'd almost reached out to her yesterday because Rorik had mentioned having kissed her and he'd somehow wanted to settle a score with his insufferable cousin. But now?

Now he had no reason to want to kiss her, not when she'd just told him she'd been lusting after all the men in the village!

"We came here so I could show you how to use a sling, remember? So shall we start?" he suggested. "After all, we didn't come here to discuss events that took place some ten years ago."

To indicate this conversation was over, he got his sling out and set about looking for suitable stones to throw. Eyja helped and soon they had assembled a sizeable heap.

"Now. Watch me."

Moon threaded his middle finger inside the loop at one end of the sling and placed one of the biggest stones in the center of it before closing his fingers around the other end of the rope. He started to rotate his wrist, then his shoulder, showing her what he was doing, breaking down his movements, making sure to go slowly so she could understand every step. Eyja found herself watching avidly, not just because she wanted to learn, but because it was fascinating. His every move was effortless, his body like a weapon itself, honed to perfection. She could have watched him all day. To think when she had spied on him as a child she had kept her eyes on the target, not on him, paying him hardly any attention, instead focusing on checking if he hit the objects he intended to hit... Now she didn't care about the result. It was the skill and beauty of the thrower that fascinated her.

Without warning he let loose of the first stone. It hit a dead branch in the tree some forty paces away. A loud crack split the air. For a moment the branch seemed to want to hang on but then it fell to the ground, defeated.

Eyja could not help a gasp. "You..."

He laughed. "What? Did you really expect me to miss such an easy target?"

"Well, no. But..." She frowned. Why was she so shocked? She had no idea. Only, the demonstration of strength and precision had somehow turned her blood to fire. "I never before realized how powerful a sling could be."

"No? Not even when you nearly took your own eye out?"

She scowled. Did he really have to remind her of her failings? "Stop talking and do that again," she said instead of answering the provocation.

Moon arched a brow and Eyja knew he was about to say he took orders from no one, much less impatient women. But then, to her surprise, he smiled—or rather smirked. "Very well. I'm yours to command, lady."

The fire in her veins raced straight to the place between her legs. If only he were hers to command... She had a few ideas of what she would ask him to do. As she could not, however, lie down on the ground and order him to lick her to ease the burn his demonstration had created within her, she nodded toward the sling pointedly.

They were here to shoot stones after all, not to indulge in scandalous acts.

After having decapitated a few plants, he handed her the sling.

"Your turn," he said, looking toward the edge of the clearing. "Try to hit that boulder over there."

The boulder in question was the size of an ox. She huffed. Was he mocking her? He'd just been using targets that were the size of her eye. "Anyone could hit that without even trying. Shouldn't we at least start with—"

"I'll decide how best it is to be done, thank you very much," he said sternly. "You asked to be shown. If we are to do this, we'll do it properly."

She surrendered. After all, she had no reason to question his ability as an instructor. He seemed to know what he was doing well enough. And indeed, to her shock, though she did her best to reproduce his movements, she missed the boulder completely. The stone sailed straight past it, scaring a bird as it disappeared into the trees.

"Mm," Moon said, not even trying to hide his amusement. "Perhaps we should have started with one the size of a house. An ox is evidently too small."

"Let me try again." She would not be defeated so easily.

After three more tries she managed to hit the center of the boulder. By the time the sun had reached its zenith, she was able to hit targets as small as a goat. Beaming, she turned to Moon.

"What do you say to that?"

He crossed his arms over his chest. "I say 'Well done.' You are a quick study. Not that I'm overly surprised, I must say."

Heat suffused her chest at the praise. "Thank you. But the merit is not all mine. You always know how to explain things in a way I can understand. I feel like I could ask you anything and you would know the answer."

It was then that she thought of something that had bothered her for days. Perhaps he had the answer. It was worth a try. After all, considering how well he knew her and what they had done together, nothing she could say would shock him.

She started hesitantly. "Moon..."

CHAPTER FOURTEEN

M oon tensed, instinct telling him this would be yet another of Eyja's questions he found impossible or awkward to answer. "What is it?" he couldn't help but ask when she stopped. If she thought it necessary to censure herself, this would be bad indeed. Nevertheless, he wanted to know.

"Farmon and Bragi both seemed interested by the idea of a woman, erm, sucking their..." She stopped and went bright red before she could repeat the rude word. "But what does it mean, exactly?"

All the blood in Moon's body rushed to the place she hadn't dared name. He imagined her on her knees in front of him, doing just that. Someone like her, wild, playful and always ready for a challenge would be perfect at giving a man such shocking pleasure. For a moment he allowed himself to get lost in the lewd image. And then fury overtook him when he remembered how Farmon had talked to her, how Bragi had grabbed her by the jaw.

"It means that they are pigs who have no idea of how to talk to or about women," he snarled.

Her face fell, as if she had expected a different answer altogether. "Oh. So... It's not something men like you would enjoy?"

Despite himself he let out a groan. Not enjoy? He would give a finger to feel the heat of a woman's mouth around his shaft at least once in his life. For all his experience, no woman had ever dared offer him this delight. "Every man, as far as I can tell, would enjoy this. I... I think I would too."

She blinked in surprise. "You mean that you've never tried? I thought you were rather experienced."

"I am." No point in pretending otherwise.

"So... why not?"

They had to stop this conversation right now. But he couldn't seem to. He was fascinated, like a vole would be in front of an eagle about to dive on him. Although only danger awaited him, he was powerless to retreat to safety.

Moon dropped the stone he'd been holding and raised his chin. Eyja wanted to talk about this? Let's see how far she was prepared to go.

"Because I've never met a woman who wanted to do it to me and it's not something I could force anyone to do," he said in a low voice. There. Not quite what he had intended to say, but honest at least.

"But the idea intrigues you?"

Oh, it did more than intrigue him, it aroused him like nothing else. He often imagined it when he gave himself pleasure at night. The answer must have shown in his eyes because she dropped her gaze to the front of his braies. Her mouth fell open when she saw how hard he was.

"I see." The imp arched a brow when all the other women he knew would most likely have gone bright red. "It does intrigue you. Perhaps... Perhaps I could do it for you."

He almost swallowed his tongue. Had she just said that? Of course, she had. She was nothing if not brazen. "Hell, Eyja, are you mad? It's not something women just offer to do to men."

She shrugged. "I don't see why not. You gave me pleasure the other day. I could do the same. Like the sling for me, it's something you've always wanted to experience. I could help you the way you helped me. Save you never knowing."

With those shocking words she closed the gap between them and wrapped her fingers around his shaft. A bolt of lightning shot straight up his spine.

"This is…" The words dried on his lips when she gave a squeeze but he forced himself to finish. "This is not the same as showing someone how to use a weapon, and you know it."

It was not even remotely the same. He should refuse.

And yet…

The offer was one he knew he might well not be able to turn down. Eyja was holding him captive with the glint in her eye and the grip of her hand around his pulsing shaft.

"You need not feel guilty, you're not forcing me to do anything. I want to do it. I think… I think I would like it as well."

Well, if she didn't render him speechless.

She gave another squeeze. He groaned. Whether he accepted or refused her offer, one thing was guaranteed. It would be the death of him. The choice was clear, if not attractive. Either be consumed by regret or racked with guilt.

"You do know what happens when a man reaches his pleasure?" But he knew she did. Thorfinn, damn the man's eyes, had shown her.

"Yes." She didn't seem to understand what he was getting at.

"If you take me in your mouth, then I will spill in your mouth." It was as simple as that and he didn't see why he should lie or even pretend that was not what he wanted. If she dared wrap her lips around him, he would hold her head in place and lose himself in the pleasure she was offering. The temptation would be impossible to resist. He would not be able to do the right thing and withdraw. He would enjoy this to the full. "I will not let you go until I've reached my release."

And it would happen more quickly than he would wish. He was already weeping with need.

"So?" Eyja looked at him from under her long lashes. "Spill in my mouth. What's wrong with that?"

So many things. "You might feel used. I don't want that. It might be uncomfortable for you. It also means you will have to swallow my seed. Every drop of it, because I won't release you until you have." He wanted to shock her, make her see the reality of what she was offering. But the imp didn't appear shocked, rather all the more fascinated. Damnation, why couldn't she be like the other women for once! A virgin should be horrified by what he was explaining, not aroused! How was he supposed to do the honorable thing when she was practically licking her lips at the idea of sucking him to completion?

"Swallow a man's seed. Is that what women do?" she asked in a throaty voice.

"I don't know," he panted. "I told you, I've never done that before. But it's what I'd want you to do and I'm not sure you'd like that."

"I'll decide what I like and how best this is to be done, thank you very much. If we are to do it, we'll do it properly," she said sternly.

The minx! She was using his earlier words against him. But why had he expected any different? She was the most vexing woman he knew. Yes, and also the fiercest, most generous one. Wasn't she offering to do something he had always fantasized about? He was quickly losing his grip on reason in front of her determination. Why was he even surprised? He should have guessed that if one woman was bold enough to introduce him to this sensual experience, it would be Eyja.

He tried to ward off temptation one last time. This was wrong, surely?

"Eyja—"

"Listen, you didn't give me any choice the other day in the forest and I ended up loving it. *I* held your head in place, *I* used you until I reached my release and I don't think you minded any of it." Oh, he had not minded it, in fact, he had loved to see that he was making her lose all restraint. "Now it's my turn to give you pleasure. It's only fair."

"That's not the way it works," he managed to rasp, feeling his thoughts scatter like twigs in a storm. His will had long since disappeared. His control was holding on by a thread.

"Since when have I done what was expected of me? You have complained about the fact often enough. Now it's time you saw it can also have its advantages. You said I was yours to command, remember? Well, this is what I want."

With those words she sank to her knees. It was no use. He would just have to surrender. And... Never had surrender been sweeter.

Slowly, she started to undo the laces at the front of his braies. He did nothing to stop her, merely watched, feeling both blessed and wretched.

"You'll have to guide me, tell me what you like," she whispered, placing her hand on his throbbing member. The feel of her fingers on his naked flesh was delicious torture.

"I-I don't know. I told you, I—"

She cut his fumbled explanations short. "Well, then, you'll just have to tell me if you like what I do."

In the end, Moon was unable to say anything. As soon as Eyja's tongue slid along his shaft, he lost the ability to think. When she closed her lips over the tip, he groaned like a man in pain. And when she engulfed him in heat, he almost collapsed to the ground.

No! He could not falter now, he had to enjoy the gift she was offering. Leaning his back against the tree for support, he let her explore, find a rhythm that suited her.

Then she moaned, the sound acting like a whiplash on his fevered brain.

Of their own accord, his hands fastened to the back of her head. Her hair was still short but not so short that he could not weave his fingers through the silky strands to hold her in place while he pushed deeper into her mouth, just as he had warned he would do. It was impossible to act differently, he had dreamed of this moment for too long, and Eyja was just too damn perfect.

"Tell me you want this," he rasped. Bloody hell, he was already too close to relief. He would have wanted this to last forever but he was going to erupt in no time. And he wanted to make the most of it while it lasted. "Tell me I can do this."

With her mouth full she couldn't answer, but the moan she gave was enough to reassure him.

Moon let go, his fingers digging into her scalp. He'd never been a shy lover but this was taking it to a new level. In a distant part of his mind, he kept listening to her moans, waiting for one that denoted protest instead of arousal, and heard nothing. Grateful beyond belief, he bucked his hips one final time.

"Fuck," was all he said before he stilled and erupted with unprecedented force.

Eyja could not understand why she was feeling so aroused. By rights, Moon should be the one experiencing desire and plea-sure, not her. And yet, her whole body was tingling. Every time he plunged inside her throat she felt the echo of the move between her legs.

He'd warned her he would use her. She hadn't understood

what he'd meant then. She did now, and she loved it. Except that she would not have called what he was doing "using her". Rather, he was making the most of the opportunity she was offering him, and allowing himself a pleasure he had always dreamed of, safe in the knowledge that she enjoyed it as well. Because her moans made that clear, and she was certain he would remember this first time as well. He would think having a woman service him thus was just as pleasurable as he had hoped for.

As for her, she would remember it as pleasurable as well. The feel of his fingers holding her in place while he slid inside her again and again was deeply erotic, as was the knowledge that for him in that moment, nothing existed than her and the warmth of her mouth.

For once he was not annoyed, or disappointed or impatient with her.

For once she was just what he needed.

He would not consider this the biggest mistake he had ever made, that was certain.

She closed her eyes and savored the moment. Never when she had carved the moon in the oak bark would she have imagined she would come here with him one day, and she would be on her knees, giving him pleasure.

He pushed inside her one last time, then he swore, and stilled. Heat flooded her mouth and, just like he'd said, she had no choice but to swallow his seed. But, unlike what he'd feared, she didn't dislike it. True, it was disconcerting at first, but the satisfaction she felt at having succeeded in making him lose his mind more than made up for it. Once he'd stopped throbbing she hummed, and to her surprise, felt him jerk one last time against her tongue. She would have smiled if she'd been able. He'd liked that then.

Slowly she released him and lifted her head up. Eyes half

closed, Moon was looking at her as if she were a supernatural apparition, one he was in awe of.

"So tell me. Am I forgiven?"

"Forgiven?" he rasped.

"For breaking your sling."

"What sling? What the hell are you talking about? The sling is intact."

A pearly laugh escaped her throat. Yes, the sling they'd just used was intact, but she meant the one she had stolen years ago. She really had reduced his brain to mush, as well as his legs to gruel if he couldn't remember their earlier conversation.

"I'll take that for a yes. Well, was it as good as you'd hoped?" she asked, heart beating hard in her chest.

He growled, and pride swelled within her. Another yes. Apparently, she'd acquitted herself of the task to his satisfaction, even though it had been her first time.

He seemed to read her mind. "You have truly never done that before?"

The question made her smile. If he doubted it, it meant she had indeed performed well. "No." With Thorfinn she had used her hand. She had not known there was an alternative and he had not asked. Which was good because she was not sure she would have liked it as much with someone else. It was a rather intimate act, she had to admit.

"I..." he started

"No. Please. Don't say you're sorry."

"I'm not." He wiped the corner of her lips with the pad of his thumb. "I know I should be but I'm not. That was—"

"—the biggest snake I'd ever seen!"

She and Moon froze and exchanged a panicked glance when the voice burst between them. A child was coming into the clearing. And not just any child, but his very young, very innocent nephew, as they understood when the boy's father's answer reached them next.

"Yes, I believe you, Gunnar," Elwyn was saying. "I only saw its tail, but it did look enormous."

No! They could not be seen together in such a provocative position. Eyja shot back to her feet while Moon hastily tucked himself back in his braies. A moment later father and son irrupted into the clearing. They came to a stop when they saw them, then the little boy ran in their direction, arms outstretched.

"Uncle Moon! Eyja! Guess what, I just saw a snake and I didn't even cry out. I was very brave!"

"Were you?"

Moon did a commendable job of sounding natural. At least to the little boy's ears. Eyja could detect a certain hoarseness in his voice and Elwyn was looking at his brother strangely, as if wondering if something was amiss. Then his gaze fell on her. She felt herself go red all the way to the roots of her hair. Had he guessed what she had just been doing to his brother? Did it somehow show in her expression? Was her hair mussed? Was her bodice lowered? Were her lips swollen?

Not knowing what else to do, she made a great show of gathering the sling and remaining stones and shoving them into the bag she'd brought along for that purpose. The little boy came to help her. He was so sweet and innocent that she could not look him in the eye in case he got a glimpse of what depravity she was capable of. Not that he had the faintest notion of what adults did together, fortunately. Even if he'd seen her kneeling in front of his uncle, he would only have assumed she was tying the lace on her shoe. The wholesome image helped restore some of her composure.

"Have you ever found yourself face to face with an enormous snake, Eyja?" he asked, his eyes sparkling with excitement.

An entirely inappropriate thought burst through her mind. Not quite a snake, but... She had once joked with Moon that he was too massive to be likened to a worm. She'd not been wrong.

"No." Somehow she forced the word through her lips.

"Well, if you do, I hope you'll be as brave as me."

"Yes, I hope so."

"What are you two doing here, so far from the village?" Moon asked Elwyn. She guessed from his tone that he too wanted to steer the conversation away from snakes because of the images it brought to his mind.

"Gunnar has been asking me to go climb the rocks on the side of the hill for months," his brother explained, gesturing at the rope slung over his shoulder. "Finally we did, but we were about to head back. What about you two?"

Thankfully the question wasn't aimed at her, for she could not have answered without stammering and blushing so much he would have known straight away something was not quite what it should be.

"Eyja wanted me to show her how to use a sling."

Oh, yes, of course, that was why they had come. She had quite forgotten about that.

Elwyn laughed. "You know, with anyone else, I would think this a pitiful lie to cover up what really happened. But with Eyja, anything is possible."

"Yes," she heard Moon say softly. "Anything."

Everything within her glowed. This was the best compliment she had ever received.

"So? Did she show any talent for it?"

Her heart skipped a beat because she knew Moon was not talking about the sling when he answered.

"Oh, yes. She's a natural."

CHAPTER FIFTEEN

W ere it not for his nephew's incessant chatter, the atmosphere might have been tense. Moon's mind was still reeling from the events of the afternoon, and his body still limp from the pleasure Eyja had coaxed from him. Had Elwyn guessed that they had been engaged in licentious activities when he had burst in on them? It was hard to tell, as he'd seemed to accept the claim that they had been practicing with the sling easily enough. There had been the jest about them covering up a lie, but that might just have been the usual banter two brothers exchanged as a matter of course. One thing was for sure, if Elwyn did believe they had come to the meadow for a tryst, it was doubtful he was imagining such a crude interlude.

Moon barely repressed a sigh. How had he allowed himself to give his desire free rein thus? Never had he treated a woman in such a way before, forgetting everything, including her comfort, in his bid to reach his pleasure. But then again, no other woman had pleasured him in that manner before, or been so generous. It was a lot easier to be assertive and selfish in such a situation.

Thankfully, the brazen imp had not taken exception to it. She had even seemed to like this side of him. Typical... No one was fiercer or bolder than she was and she'd always enjoyed being treated as an equal who did not need to be cosseted.

Bedding her would be explosive, he was as sure of it as he was of his ability to hit an ox-size target with a sling. And now that he knew it... How was he going to resist putting the theory to the test? They had already given each other pleasure with their mouths, perhaps the most intimate act two people could share. After that, lying together would only be—

"Look at those flowers!"

The little boy, probably tired of extracting more than three words at a time from the adults, started to run ahead to explore his surroundings. Moon prayed his nephew would not see even the tip of a snake's tail. He would not be able to endure another discussion about what Eyja would do when faced with a snake, because he knew only too well what she would do.

Swallow it whole.

He groaned when his groin tightened at the thought. Damn it, this wouldn't do!

Gunnar pointed to a yellow patch in the distance. "I want to get some of those for Mama."

"All right, son, but don't go any farther than that, I need to be able to see—"

Before Elwyn could finish his sentence, the little boy vanished in front of their eyes. The three of them froze. What on earth had happened?

They darted forward at the same time and quickly found themselves on the edge of a crevice that had been hidden by vegetation. It was obvious the little boy had not seen it either, and simply slipped inside the crack. That was why it had appeared as if he'd been swallowed up by the ground. Because he had, in a way.

"Gunnar!" Elwyn's shout was unlike anything Moon had ever heard. Not that he could blame his brother for panicking. His own heart had given a jolt when he'd seen his nephew disappear into the crevice. He could not imagine how he would feel if it had been his son. "Can you hear me? Are you hurt? Answer me."

"Father?" The little voice, hesitant though it was, sent blood pumping back through Moon's veins. The boy was alive, at least. Was he injured?

"Are you all right, son?"

"Yes, there are leaves everywhere here. It's soft."

Moon exchanged a glance with his brother and both of them visibly relaxed. It could have been so much worse.

"Can you move, Gunnar, wave to me?"

They saw a white little hand flutter in the darkness, much closer than they had first dreaded. The hole seemed to be no more than fifteen feet deep. It would be easy enough for himself or Elwyn to jump down there without hurting themselves. Except... Except that there was no way a fully grown man could fit through the crevice where the little boy had slipped. It was just too narrow. Moon could almost span it with two hands.

"We could throw him the rope you used for climbing the rocks to haul him up," he suggested, nodding toward the rope wrapped around his brother's chest. "But I'm afraid he won't be strong enough to hold on while we hoist him up in the air. And if he lets go..." He didn't finish the sentence but there was no need. If the little boy fell from such a height a second time, this time on his back, he might not survive the drop. They had been lucky once, they might not be so lucky twice. It was obvious from the way Elwyn's jaw tightened that he was thinking the same thing.

What could they do? Could they perhaps—

"Let me go down."

They turned around as one.

"Eyja?" Elwyn said, as if he'd forgotten she was even here.

"I'm small enough to fit through the crack, I think." She glanced down, as if to evaluate the width of it. Yes, Moon agreed, *she* might fit inside. Just about. "Once I'm in the hole I'll be able to wrap the rope around Gunnar's waist and hoist him up at least part of the way while you lift him and I'll be there to catch him if he falls. Then once he's out you'll haul me back up in turn."

The two brothers looked at each other.

"She's right. It's the only solution," Elwyn said eventually.

It was. Still, Moon hesitated. Without knowing why, he didn't like the idea of her in that dark pit.

"Please, let me go. I hate the idea of Gunnar being all alone down there in the dark, scared, when I know I can help. "

That decided him. If she was brave enough to attempt the rescue, he would not stop her.

While the two men untangled the rope, Eyja knelt by the crevice to examine it while she talked to the little boy. "I'm coming down to get you now, Gunnar. Can you wait a little longer? We'll get you out in no time."

The little voice coming from underneath seized her gut. "Yes. I'll be brave. Like I was with the snake."

"Of course you will. I trust you. Good boy."

The hole appeared to be no more than fifteen feet deep. Holding on to a rope, hauled by two strapping men, the little boy would be out in no time. As for herself, she wasn't worried. If she could go in, she would be able to go out.

"Here."

She stood back up, eyeing the rope Elwyn was handing out to her. He had tied a loop at one end.

"Put your foot here and hold on to the rope," he instructed.

"We'll lower you down. It's better than you jumping down and twisting your ankle when you land on soft ground."

She nodded. The whole point was for her to reach the bottom unscathed, so she could help the little boy. This was an ingenious way of ensuring she did. "Very well."

"And, Eyja? Thank you."

The expression on her friend's face had never been more intense. Moved, she gave him a small smile. "You can thank me when I come back. Let's get Gunnar out first."

She sat down with her legs dangling over the ledge and sighed. It would be a tight fit, even if she'd always been on the slender side, she was not quite the same size as a small child. As if to prove it, her buttocks soon got stuck. Nevertheless, it was not enough to make her lose all hope of fitting through the crack. She wiggled and bit back a groan when a sharp piece of rock ripped along her hip bone. It stung something fierce and would most likely bleed, but at least the hardest part was done. She was through. Her stomach was flat and her bosom, which had never been very generous, would pose no difficulty.

Indeed it didn't and soon she was dangling in the air. The men, who must have felt the jolt on the rope, started to lower her down slowly. Almost immediately she felt the ground under her feet. It was, like Gunnar had said, soft and carpeted in leaves.

"I'm down!" she shouted to the men, even if they had probably felt the slackening of the rope.

Disentangling her foot from the loop, she knelt down and took Gunnar in her arms.

"It's over. We'll soon get you out of here," she murmured in his ear. "Your father is waiting for you up there." The little boy nodded against her neck and she wondered for a moment if he was not crying. But, of course, being brave, he would never allow her to see it. So she simply held him and pretended not to notice the wetness on her skin.

"Have you got him?" Elwyn's voice reached her.

"Yes. He's all right. I will tie the rope around his waist and chest and explain to him what he has to do."

Once she'd explained the plan to Gunnar, she told him to hold on as tight as he could while the men hoisted him up. Then she lifted him up into her arms and gave him a kiss before calling out to the men to start pulling. A moment later she felt the little boy leave her arms. He disappeared through the crack and soon she heard his father's voice, gruff with relief.

"Gunnar. Good boy. I'm here."

Eyja hugged herself and wiped a tear from her eye.

"Are you all right?" Moon's face appeared at the edge of the crevice.

"Yes."

"Hold on, we'll send you the rope in a moment."

While she waited for the men to untie and reassure the little boy, Eyja looked around and saw that she was not, contrary to what she had first believed, in a closed chamber. There was an opening to her left that seemed to lead into some sort of tunnel. Perhaps she could leave that way, instead of being lifted through the crevice? Or perhaps it was only a cavity that led to another enclosed space. Even if it did lead out, it might become too low for her to use, or be miles long and take her somewhere she would not recognize. It would also be dark and she didn't have any light with her. No. Better to stick to their original solution, even if she dreaded the moment she would have to squeeze through the narrow, sharp gap again. For sure it would cost her another nasty cut to the hip. The first one was still throbbing. Oh well. At least it would be over in a moment, and cuts healed. She knew that better than most.

The important thing was that the little boy was out and safe.

Presently, the rope was thrown to her. She wrapped it around her waist and chest much as she had done for Gunnar, tied the knot securely and placed her foot in the loop. The two brothers would be strong enough to haul her up but, unlike the little boy had done, she decided she would put her feet on the wall while they did. It would stop her from dangling helplessly in mid-air.

"I'm ready!" she called, taking a firm hold on the rope.

There. She would be out in no time at all.

IT ALL HAPPENED in the blink of an eye.

One moment Eyja was climbing, and everything was going well. The next, Moon felt a jolt, and the rope went down a few inches, as if someone had tugged on it. When he heard a dull thud, he understood what had happened. A piece of rock had been dislodged by the rubbing of the rope over the ledge and fallen down.

Right where Eyja was.

Holding on for dear life, he approached the hole carefully. Was the whole thing about to crumble under his feet? "Eyja!" he shouted, looking over the edge.

No answer. She was dangling limply, suspended by the rope she had been smart enough to wrap around her chest. It was a frightening sight but at least she hadn't fallen flat on her back.

"Lower her down!" he cried to his brother. "Gently." The last thing he wanted was for her to hit the bottom hard and damage herself further.

They soon felt the rope slacken, indicating she was now lying at the bottom of the crevice. He knelt by the edge again and peered inside.

"Eyja!" he called again, his voice little more than a terrified bark.

Nothing.

She was lying on the soft leaves, utterly still, arms flayed, legs akimbo. The stone hitting her skull had knocked her cold and now... Now he didn't know if she was still alive. Fear such as he had never known gripped his guts. Even when he'd faced the invading Norse army he had not felt this icy cold in his middle.

"We have to get to her! Now!"

Elwyn put a hand over his shoulder. "We can't. You know we can't fit through the crack. If we could, I would have gone down there myself to get Gunnar."

"We can make it bigger. If it's falling apart anyway, it shouldn't be too difficult. We could—"

"No. We cannot risk having any of the falling rocks hitting her."

His brother was right. Of course, he was right. They could not afford to hurt her if there was any chance she was still alive, they could not bury her under the rubble falling from the ledge.

Moon tore at his hair in powerlessness. How had it come to this? Only earlier this afternoon they had been in the clearing together, locked in the most intimate of embraces, and now he was wondering if she was still breathing. What would he do if she was dead? How would he face her family? How would *he* bear it?

"We have to do something!" he cried out. "We can't just stand there!"

"Why don't you use the other entrance to get to the girl?"

For a moment Moon didn't understand why Elwyn's voice had become so nasal. Then the meaning of the words hit him. "What do you mean? What other entrance?"

He turned and found himself face-to-face with a stranger.

Of course, *he* had spoken in the nasal voice. But where on earth had he sprung from? And who was he?

"Forgive me," the man said before Moon could ask any of the questions jostling in his mind. "I could not help overhearing you and it seems to me that you—"

"You know of another way of accessing the cave, then?" Elwyn cut in.

"Oh, aye, though not many do, I daresay." The man chuckled as if the situation was amusing. It wasn't, not in the least. "I know that because one of my son's goats got herself trapped in that very hole one day. It was his prized beast so naturally we wanted to—"

"Will you show us where the entrance is?" It was Moon's turn to interrupt him. He was not even remotely interested in the goat right now. He just wanted to go to Eyja.

"Of course. It is well hidden but my memory doesn't fail me."

They followed the man down the slope and round the hillock. Moon was doing his best not to let his impatience show. It was not his fault the man moved at the pace of a snail, as he was old enough to be his grandfather, but still, he could feel his nerves slowly being ripped to shreds. Finally, after what felt like an eternity, they stopped in front of an unassuming boulder.

"Here. If you move the vines and brambles, you will access the tunnel. It's been years since anyone has used it by the looks of things, but with luck it will still be clear."

The two brothers started to tear the vegetation apart, heedless of the thorns clawing at their flesh. Against all odds they had been allowed a way to get to Eyja. It was all that mattered.

"Will I be able to stand to get to where my friend is?" Moon asked the man when the way was finally clear. It would be of little use if he had to crawl to reach Eyja, for then how would he get her out? He could not shove her or drag her through a tunnel for yards on end.

The man cackled. Moon almost snarled at him. Why the *hell* did he think this was amusing? "A strapping lad like you will have to stoop in a few places, for sure, but you should be fine. Even better, you will see where you're going as it is not so long and rather straight. There's only a short section in the middle where you might have to grope around to find your way."

Elwyn nodded to him. "Will you be able to carry her on your own? Shall I come with you?"

"No." He would get her out, if it killed him. "You stay here with Gunnar."

Without wasting another moment, Moon ran inside. It seemed to take him forever and he did have to stoop in places and grope around in the middle of the tunnel, as the man had warned, but eventually he found himself in the small chamber.

"Eyja!" he cried, falling to his knees next to her.

Her position was still as unnatural as that of a dislocated skeleton. She hadn't moved an inch the whole time it had taken him to reach her. Panicked, he brought his face to her mouth and nose and felt her breath against his cheek. Alive, thank the gods. He was only very marginally reassured, however, because she was in a pitiful state. There was a deep cut to the side of her head and her dress was ripped at the hip, the skin underneath, torn and bleeding.

"Eyja!" he repeated urgently. How long had she been unconscious now? Too long for comfort. "Can you hear me? Imp, wake up. Please. Now is not the moment to be contrary, do you hear? Just... wake up!"

He carried on shaking her by the shoulder, careful not to jolt her too much. After a moment, she started stirring.

"Moon?"

Relief almost floored him. She was not dead. She could talk. She had recognized him. Perhaps he could start to hope. "Hush. Don't talk. I'll get you out of here. I will carry you and we'll get you home. Everything will be fine. I'm here."

Gently, he lifted her into his arms. His heart skipped a beat when she did not protest at this treatment. The usually brash, indomitable woman lay against his chest as calmly as a sleeping babe. Oh, this was not good. What would he not give in this moment to have her swat his arm or snarl at him the way she often did!

Without a word, he entered the tunnel again. His progress was much slower than he would have liked, as it he didn't want to risk knocking her against the walls and he had to feel for the way with an extended leg in the dark section. But still he plodded on.

"When we get out of here I swear I'm never going to—"

He stopped, not quite knowing what he had meant to say.

By the time they exited into the light again, he found a horse and cart waiting for them. Elwyn had cajoled the old man, who didn't live far, into lending them what they needed to take Eyja back to the village. Grateful beyond words, for he wanted to get her seen by the healer as soon as possible, Moon settled her in the back, holding her securely in his lap while his brother drove on.

Once they were off, he allowed the back of his head to rest against the side of the cart and let out a long, shuddering breath. What had just happened?

Life with Eyja, always somewhat unpredictable, had gone downright hectic of late and he could hardly keep up. In the past month, they had walked to the other end of the country, faced an army of invaders, fought and survived a battle to the death, shared intimacies only lovers shared and almost been forced to wed.

Today had been another example of how things went between them. One moment he was teaching her how to throw stones with a sling, the next he was emptying all he had into her mouth. Then, before he'd had time to recover from the shattering release, he'd had to watch her rescue his nephew and almost die in the process.

No one he knew could have made him experience such a dizzying series of events in such short a time and he wasn't sure how his heart was supposed to deal with it all. The imp might well lead him to an early grave at this rate.

Everything had been turned on its head and now he didn't know what to do or think.

In the last few weeks he had discovered someone he had known all his life. He'd seen her in a man's garb and, ironically, it had made him realize that she was more woman than all his other conquests put together, more fascinating, more essential to him. Lovers came and went, but she was the only constant. He'd started bedding women some ten years ago but she had been there from the beginning. It struck him that he wanted her to be there till the end as well.

Being with her was as natural as breathing, soothing, as in her presence he didn't have to pretend or hide what he thought. She knew him for the man he was, and still liked him. This acceptance seemed like the greatest gift anyone had ever given him. With her, there was no calculation, no constant efforts, no pretence, just pleasure and peace of mind.

His hold around her tightened.

She had to make it, she simply had to.

CHAPTER SIXTEEN

"Take Eyja home and get her settled while I go get Helga to see to her injuries," Elwyn instructed as he steered the cart into the village.

Moon nodded, daunted by the prospect of having to explain to her parents what had happened to her. Wolf would be mad, and it was hard to blame him.

Holding her tight, he knocked on the door. No point in delaying the inevitable.

"Oh! Eyja! Dear God, what happened?"

To his relief, only her mother was home. He would have hated to face the Icelander whilst holding his half-conscious, bleeding daughter in his arms. This time he might not have exited the hut in one piece. Two weeks ago he had brought her back home from war, then he had gotten involved in a village brawl over her. Now, once again, the man's daughter was in danger, and, once again, he was involved. Wolf might well come to the conclusion that their being together meant trouble.

He deposited her onto the pallet before explaining to Merewen what had happened. She listened while bathing the wound on her daughter's temple with careful gestures. Moon's chest constricted. The wound was horrific and would most likely leave a scar, but that was not what worried him. All the while Eyja barely opened her eyes and mumbled unintelligible words. She seemed barely aware of her surroundings.

A moment later, Helga, the healer, entered the hut. She looked straight toward the pallet and nodded.

"Elwyn told me this young lady requires my services. A blow to the head, is it?"

"Yes."

Merewen started to explain what had happened. Feeling like an intruder, Moon slipped out of the hut but waited outside, determined to ask the healer what her opinion was when she came back out again. He had never seen Eyja so subdued in his life, and he hated it. She was usually so vibrant, so full of life... Would she ever recover?

To his relief, it was not long before the door opened again. He all but pounced on the healer.

"How is she?"

"Moon!" She gave him a shaky smile. "By the gods, you made me jump, boy!"

"Forgive me." It was hard to be patient when his nerves had been ripped to shreds. "I didn't mean to scare you. How is Eyja?" he repeated.

Helga didn't appear worried when she answered, which eased his anguish somewhat. "She will be fine, once the headache has cleared. I gave her a potion so she can try and sleep the worst of it off. After a good night's rest, she should start to feel like her usual self again. Worry not. She's not as frail as she appears to be, that one, but I suspect I don't need to tell you that."

"No." Indeed, the imp was one of the toughest people he knew. She had proved it time and time again. His breathing slowed down at last. Maybe everything would be all right. "Thank you."

"No problem. Try not to worry too much."

Easier said than done. "Will I be able to see her when she wakes up?"

The older woman looked at him curiously. "Is there a reason why you should not?"

The question took him by surprise. Was there? Yes, perhaps, but not one he could share with anyone.

"I suppose it depends on who you ask," he grumbled in a bid at honesty. Her father might not be best pleased to see him visit, and Eyja herself might prefer to be allowed some time to mull over all that had happened in the afternoon.

Helga only laughed. "Well, until you are expressly forbidden to, I would say there is no reason for you not to see her. She's already asked for you anyway, one of the few intelligible things she said."

Moon's heart skipped a beat. Eyja had asked after him? Gratefulness invaded him. In spite of all, she still wanted to see him. Well, as long as she wanted to see him, he would see her.

"Thank you. She... She's very precious to me."

The same thing he had told Cuthbert. It now seemed truer than ever.

"Apparently." The woman smiled. "Now go home and have a rest. You look about to drop off."

It was then that Moon realized he was done for. After a brief nod to the healer, he walked back to his hut. There he removed his boots, fell onto his pallet and closed his eyes, determined to be back first thing in the morning.

"WHERE AM I?" Eyja's voice was little more than a whisper and her head was as heavy as if it had been filled with rocks. She could not really focus and her body ached all over. Why was that?

"You're at home." Her mother's voice reached her from the other side of the hut. Soon, she was by her side, kneeling by the pallet. There was an uncertain smile on her lips, as if she weren't certain of the welcome she would get. "You slept all night and for the best part of the morning. How do you feel? Do you remember what happened yesterday?"

Yesterday. The word caused Eyja to sit bolt upright—or at least try to, because as soon as she moved, her skull exploded. But, yes, she did remember. Everything. Moon. The clearing, the sling, the shocking pleasure she'd given him.

The pleasure it had given her.

"Yesterday?" she croaked.

How did her mother know about that? Surely Moon had not told her what they had done together while she slept, oblivious to it all? No, he would not have. But who then? Elwyn? Had he mentioned walking in on them in the clearing? Or was it even worse than that? Had her friend actually seen them, like Farmon had seen them that morning in the forest? It was not impossible. But why mention such a private thing to her mother? She could not make sense of any of it, especially with her head throbbing the way it was.

"Moon brought you back home yesterday evening, looking like a shadow of his usual self. The poor man is racked with guilt over it all, and I had to assure him no one would even think of blaming him. These things happen and no one forced you to do it." The hand holding her gave a squeeze. "I'm proud of you, daughter."

Eyja blinked. She was *proud*? Had she heard that right?

"What did Moon tell you exactly?" she asked cautiously. She wasn't sure she was ready to hear it but something wasn't right. She could well believe that Moon felt guilty over using her, as he'd called it, for his pleasure, but her mother congratulating her for kneeling at a man's feet? It made no sense.

"Everything, how you volunteered when it became clear no one else could do it." Eyja's insides withered. He had even told her mother that she had been the first one to offer to pleasure him in that shocking manner? What on earth had possessed him to do such a thing? She would make sure to tell him what she thought of it the next time she saw him.

"I can't believe he told you about it," she whispered. "You're not... mad?"

"Mad? Of course, not! If you mean that your father and I don't always approve of your recklessness, it's true we sometimes fear for you, but this is quite different. I'm sure I would have done the same thing in your place."

"Please. I'm not sure I..."

She was not quite comfortable discussing such a thing with her mother but her protests fell on deaf ears.

"I mean, what else could you have done? That poor little boy! How else were you supposed to get him out of the hole?"

The hole. Gunnar.

Of course, *that* was what her mother was talking about, not what she had done to Moon at the foot of the oak. Eyja could have kicked herself. She really was the stupidest girl who'd ever lived. And how had she forgotten about the incident in the crevice? Weren't her aching body and thick head enough to remind her of it? Then she spotted a vial of brown liquid on the table. Helga's potion, notoriously potent and to be handled with caution. No doubt it was responsible for the momentary lapse in memory.

"Well, I had no other choice," she told her mother, doing her best to appear as if she had not only just now understood what they were talking about. "I could not bear to see poor Gunnar on his own in that hole. As you said, anyone who could would have done the same."

"Yes. How do you feel now?"

"The wound still stings something awful, and my head is all hazy. But I'm sure I will be fine." Eyja looked around while her mother stood back up and brought her a cup of ale to drink. "Where is *Faðir*?"

"He's gone into town for a few days."

She was relieved to hear it, as it was for the best he had not seen her brought back to the hut injured and bleeding. She had a feeling he would blame Moon for it, even if this time it had nothing to do with him. Of course, he would still hear about it when he came back but by then the worst would be over and she would look more presentable. It was better that he only saw her once her wound had had time to heal a bit.

Just then a knock sounded at the door.

"Moon," her mother said when she opened. "Please come in. I was on my way to fetch some water. You can keep Eyja company while I'm gone."

The ploy to leave them alone was blatant but Eyja was grateful. She needed to have a private word with him. Not to berate him for revealing to her mother what they had done, though, as she had first imagined she would. She afforded a smile when she imagined his reaction if she'd hinted at the fact that he'd spoken about it. He would rightly be horrified.

"How do you feel?" he asked, coming closer to the pallet where she was sitting.

She brushed her temple. "Not wonderful but better."

"And the other cut?" He glanced at her lower body, which

was still covered with the blanket. She was both touched that he should remember the insignificant wound.

"It was never an issue. The gap was narrower than I thought, that's all, and it scraped my hip as I went down."

He nodded, as if satisfied. "I cannot thank you enough for what you did for my nephew."

Eyja waved the thanks away, which did not surprise Moon. In truth, though he was genuinely grateful for what she'd done, he knew it would offend her to insist, since she had done nothing more than anyone would have done in her place. She had been the only one who could help, and she had done so. It was that simple, and to suggest otherwise would suggest that he didn't think her capable of basic human decency, which he did not.

Besides, he did not doubt Gunnar's parents would soon visit to thank her properly, as was their place. He was only the boy's uncle and that was not why he was here.

"I don't think you came here to thank me for getting into that hole," she said slowly, as if reading his mind.

He shook his head. She was right and he didn't see why he should pretend otherwise. The sooner he got this over, the better, because his stomach was already churning. He had done a lot of thinking about the future since waking up at dawn, and he needed to get it all off his chest.

"I think... I think we should forget about what happened these last few weeks."

Eyja stilled then gave a sigh, as if she'd pondered the same thing and agreed. "I already have. I've learned my lesson and do not intend to go to war ever again. Anyway, it's probably too late, by now King Harold's army will have—"

"Please," Moon cut in. Indeed, there was no point worrying about her fleeing to join the army. By now the Normans would either be defeated, or King Harold would be dead. But that was not what he was worried about, and she knew it. The imp was deliberately misunderstanding him. He should have guessed it would not be that easy. "I'm not talking about the battle at Stamford Bridge and well you know it."

He threw her a stern stare. She blushed, caught red-handed. "I do know it. But *that*, I don't want to forget about. I'm not even sure I can."

Neither was he, which was the whole problem.

"No. But we must." He would go mad if they didn't. He had not slept well the night before and he anticipated many more nights spent torturing himself with the memory of the taste and sounds of her arousal. As for the feel of her sweet lips wrapped around him, he would think about it every time he stroked himself for the rest of his life and the thought sat ill with him. "I can't use you again the way I did." He gestured at her head, which was heavily bandaged. How scared he had been to see her bleeding, limp form at the bottom of the crevice! "I can't bear to see you hurt again."

Eyja placed a hand over her temple, then on his forearm. "This injury has nothing to do with what... with what we did in the clearing," she whispered. "And well you know it."

The impudent little imp was repeating his earlier words to him. And on principle, she was right. But Moon was not in the mood to be fair or reasonable. He just wanted this discussion to be over.

"If we hadn't been in that clearing in the first place, none of this would have happened. Gunnar would not have gone anywhere near the crevice as we wouldn't have been with him and Elwyn."

Though that was indisputable, she was not so easily cowered. "We went there because I wanted you to show me how to use a sling, not because I intended to..." Her voice trailed away and she reddened.

Not because I intended to make you lose your mind by taking you in my mouth.

The words never passed her lips but he understood well enough.

"I know. Still," he groaned. Everything was mixed up in his head. He had to bring an end to that discussion, he had to leave this hut with the assurance that they would put an end to this madness and be friends again. "It's been a crazy few weeks but we need things to go back to normal. I can't deal with anything else."

She shook her head slowly, almost regretfully, as if she wanted to agree with him, but could not. "It's not about what we want, Moon. We cannot undo what has been done, or wish away how we feel."

No. Unfortunately.

Then he blinked as the words hit him. How they *felt?* What was Eyja saying? This was not about how they felt, but about what they had done, nothing more. He wasn't questioning the workings of his mind, he only regretted what his bodily urges had made him do, which was not the same at all. He didn't feel any different, he only wished he could act the way he should toward someone who was a friend, not a lover.

But he could not insist, explain that he had only given in to crude masculine desires, admit that he would have surrendered to any woman who offered to pleasure him on her knees because then she would feel like a whore, and he didn't want that. Still, deep down, he knew the truth. He hadn't agreed to use her mouth because she was Eyja and he had feelings for her, only because she was a woman and she had been willing.

Without a doubt, she wouldn't like to hear that.

He stood up with decision. "I would be grateful if you give

what I said some consideration and see that it is the best way forward."

"For whom?"

"For both of us." He clenched his jaw, holding on to his decision. It was the best decision, he reminded himself, the only honorable one. They were friends, nothing more. It was time they remembered that. "I will leave you to rest now. You need it."

Well, Eyja reflected bitterly as the door closed on Moon. At least this time he had not called what they had done the biggest mistake of his life. As consolations went, it was a small one.

She fell back on the pallet, pensively. Moon wanted them to forget what had happened and go back to the way they had been before. Even if that was what she had wanted—which it was not —how was she supposed to do that? Things *were* different now, and acts, especially intimate ones like the caresses they had shared, had consequences. Her hair would eventually grow back to its usual length, but she wasn't sure there was such a thing as normal for them anymore.

Later that morning she had other visitors. Bee and Gunnar entered moments after she had finished getting dressed.

The little boy threw himself into her arms as soon as he saw her. "Thank you, Eyja, you saved me."

Eyja closed her arms around him, kneeling to embrace him better. "You're welcome, Gunnar. I could not be less brave than you, now, could I?"

He grinned and shook his little head. "I brought you some flowers to thank you for coming to get me in the pit."

He handed her a small, somewhat crumpled bunch of hare-bells. Her throat tightened. The way he was clutching the blue flowers was so adorable she wanted to cry. Or perhaps she just wanted to cry because there had been a lump in her throat since

Moon had left the hut, a lump she had refused to acknowledge, in the hope that it would eventually go away.

It had not.

It might not for a long time, if ever.

"Thank you. They're beautiful."

Looking concerned at the wobble in her voice, the little boy placed a finger over her bruise. "Are you in pain? You look like a warrior back from battle, you know."

She had to smile at that, because ironically, she had come back from war unscathed and, now that she was safe, back to her normal life, she did look as if she'd been battling fierce enemies. "I do?"

"You do. You said you would be brave if you ever saw a snake. Well, now I know you would. You've proved it."

Not the snake again! Would she ever be able to hear that word without thinking of Moon and what they had done together? Probably not. Fortunately, Bee spoke before she could blush to the roots of her hair.

"Elwyn and I are very grateful for what you did for our son. I don't know how to thank you."

There was such emotion in her friend's voice that Eyja felt her chest tighten again. Could she indulge in a bout of crying that might make her feel better? No one would think it odd if she finally freed herself of the sobs that had been building in her throat all morning, putting them down to the emotion of the moment.

"Please," she whispered, deciding it was best not to cry. If she started, there was no saying when or if she would be able to stop. "'Tis nothing. And all is well that ends well, so we'll speak no more of it."

Bee gave her hand a squeeze. "Of course."

After one last kiss, mother and son left.

Moon's younger sister, Aife, came to visit as Eyja and her mother were finishing their meat pastries.

The two of them had always been quite close but since she had come back from battle, or more to the point since she had become intimate with her brother, Eyja had been feeling quite uncomfortable in front of her friend. It would be even worse now, she guessed. Forget the liberty Moon had taken with her, what would his sister think if she knew what Eyja had done to *him*? Knew that she had been the one initiating it? He'd alluded to the fact that this was not something women usually offered to do, thereby implying that it was particularly wicked, or even possibly forbidden. The fact that he had never experienced it alone proved that it was not as common a practice as men would have liked.

"How do you feel?" Aife asked, oblivious to her lewd musings.

"Fine," she murmured. Physically at least, she felt fine. The rest was more complicated.

"That reminds me, it is time to check the wound," her mother said. "Helga will want to know how it's healing."

She unwrapped the bandages and bathed the wound before declaring herself satisfied. Aife looked on, then cocked her head in consideration when they left the wound to dry out.

"You know, your scar is exactly the same shape and size as Moon's birth mark. Why, it's unbelievable how similar they look. It will fade to white with time, I imagine, but at the moment it's almost the same color as his, as well." She shook her head, amused. "It's funny, really."

It was not funny at all. Eyja felt as if she'd been branded, marked as his. It was as if she were now his for all to see. Except... Except that she was not, and would never be. He didn't want her in that way, he'd told her as much only this morning. He felt guilty over what they had done, and made it clear he would never touch her again or agree to her lewd propositions. And where did that leave her? Because she craved his touch and she knew she would not stop fantasizing about all the things she could do to him, just because it was more convenient.

He'd decreed they should forget about what they had done without consulting with her first or even asking himself if such a thing were possible.

She wasn't sure it was.

When Aife left, she pretended to have a headache to be allowed to go to bed. Her mother looked at her strangely but did not ask any questions. It took Eyja a long time to fall asleep.

The next morning a heavy mist wrapped over the land, which did not help with her sense of despondency. All day she wandered aimlessly between the hut and the vegetable patch, not knowing what to do with herself. She thought back to her idea of moving houses. Could she really build her own hut, with some help from her family? The idea had merit, now more than ever. Having something to occupy her hands might help her steer her mind from thoughts of Moon, give her the illusion she was not wasting away while waiting for him to change his mind. In time, she might manage to make him believe she had done what he'd asked and forgotten all about him.

It would only be pretend, though. Forgetting what they had done not only seemed impossible, but it was the last thing she wanted to do. She wanted to relive it over and over again.

That evening, her father came back from town.

As soon as he saw the bruise on her temple, he came to a halt and roared, just as she had predicted he would.

"Who dared—"

"Calm down, Wolf," her mother interposed, placing a hand over his arm. "There was an accident, this is no one's fault."

She started to explain what had happened in a soothing voice. When Moon's name was mentioned, Eyja saw in the tightening in her father's jaw that, one way or the other, he would find a way to place the blame on him. He would tell her that if they hadn't gone into the woods together, she would have been nowhere near that crevice, or he would claim that Moon should have investigated about a possible other entrance before sending her down the hole. Nothing would be too far-fetched, as long as it painted Moon in a bad light. It was both ridiculous and unworthy of the man he was.

"Can I speak to you alone, *Faðir*?" she asked, doing her best to remain calm. Now was not the time to let her tongue run away with her.

"Of course."

Before leaving, her mother threw her husband a look Eyja had difficulty interpreting. She might have been warning him to be gentle, or indicating that she agreed with everything he would say. There just was no telling.

The door closed silently.

Not seeing any point in prevaricating, Eyja simply asked what she wanted to ask. "Why did you want me to marry Moon if you think him so untrustworthy?"

"I don't think him untrustworthy," was the infuriating response. She could scarce believe it. Since they had come back from war, he had not uttered a single good thing about "Half-dan", accusing him of all sorts of deeds.

"Do you not?" she scoffed. "Then at least admit you don't trust him to be around me. And another thing. Did you really want me to marry against my will?" she added before her father could contradict her or she could lose her nerve.

It was hard to hide her disappointment and anger at the thought. Up until her return from York she had assumed her father loved her and wanted the best for her. She had not been impressed to find out that he'd been ready to force her into a marriage he'd not even discussed with her beforehand.

"I would never have you do anything against your will, least of all marry a man who doesn't deserve you," was his answer.

"But you said—"

"I said you should marry him if you were with child. Because then I would have known it wasn't against your will." When she arched a brow, he explained. "To carry his child, you'd have to have lain with the man."

She could not believe it. Days after she'd proven she was not lying, they were back to the same argument. Was she wasting her time? "I told you we never slept together!"

"Yes. But if you had, it would have been because you wanted it. I know how opinionated you can be and I've known Halfdan since he was born. He would never—"

"Stop calling him Halfdan!" She hated it, hated the disapproval it represented. But her father ignored her protest and carried on.

"He would never have forced you. This, at least, I believe. So it follows that this encounter, or encounters, could only have happened with your consent, if not at your request." She tried very hard not to blush because that was exactly what had happened. *She* had been the one provoking Moon, pushing him over the edge, both times. Her father really knew her too well. "For you to do that would mean that you felt something for the lad, even if you weren't fully conscious of it at the time. And for you to feel something for him meant that you thought him worthy of interest and deserving of you. You would therefore have found yourself married to man you had chosen for his qualities, a man you desired enough to give yourself to, a man you've always known and liked, the father of your child. There are worst starts to a marriage."

This explanation and the logic behind it, left Eyja speechless.

He was right. Her sleeping with Moon would have proved

she was not indifferent to him as a man, and them having grown together meant they knew what to expect from one another as husband and wife. Many marriages indeed had less promising starts, she had already come to that conclusion herself. She could not surrender so quickly, however. He would have left her no choice in a decision that would have affected her whole life. This was not so easy to forgive.

"Choosing to sleep with a man and marrying him are two different things, I would say. One doesn't necessarily have to follow after the other."

"It does if there is a child!" He made a cutting gesture with his hand. "I would never have my daughter raising a child without the help and support she is entitled to, or my grandchild growing without its father, and I will not apologize for it. Halfdan would have had to face his responsibilities because there are ways to prevent a pregnancy, things a man of honor can do to protect the woman he is bedding from the consequences of their actions. But now that I know for sure that you are not with child, we can forget all about it, if such is your wish."

Eyja noticed that he hadn't said: "now that I know Moon didn't touch you", as if he knew they had shared intimacies. Perhaps her mother had hinted at their discussion together. Her parents had no secrets from each other. But she didn't mind. Her father cared for her, that was the important thing. Her mother had been right. He had never meant to force her into anything, merely to protect her and her child and force Moon to do the right thing by her. Not only that, but he'd understood that she had feelings for the vexing man long before she had.

"How about him?" she couldn't help but ask. Perhaps her perceptive father had useful insight into what Moon thought. Perhaps he could give her the ray of light she desperately needed after their conversation the previous day.

"What do you mean?"

"You said you thought I might have feelings for Moon. Do you think he... feels anything for me?"

Please say yes. Please say I'm not a fool for lusting after him, for wanting to be more than friends. Please say he will change his mind.

There was a pause.

"Ask him who chose the family's horse's name."

She blinked. What did that have to do with anything?

A few years ago, her father's beloved stallion, Demon, had died. The black horse he had sired on their mare, Angel, which had turned out to be the last he was to have, had been gifted to Sigurd when he'd been a year old. It looked exactly like its formidable father, and had been called Imp. Eyja had always assumed it was because people liked to give the stallion's offspring names that echoed Demon's. The village was now populated with Devils, Ghouls and all kinds of Norse deities.

Caedmon was the only one who had broken the unspoken rule, calling his mare Sapphire after his favorite gem, and his wife Ingrid's eye color.

"Do you mean Demon's last foal?" she asked her father.

"Yes."

She still didn't see what that might have to do with Moon's feelings. But her curiosity had definitely been piqued and she knew she would ask about the horse's name the first chance she got.

"Wolf, your wife told me you were back," Magnus, the smithy called out through the window. "Do you have a moment? Someone's here to see you."

Her father ran a hand through his hair. Just like her mother's, it was streaked with silver now. And just like her, he had never looked better. "Will you forgive me?"

"Of course." All her life she had seen him answer to others' solicitations. His life had been at the service of the villagers long before she'd been born, ever since he'd arrived from Iceland thirty years ago. Eyja was used to it. "Thank you. For everything."

She fell into his arms and finally gave way to the sobs she had been holding off for two days.

"I love you, daughter. I want only the best for you. Never doubt it."

Eyja's throat tightened. "I won't."

CHAPTER SEVENTEEN

"Where is Imp?"

Moon arched a brow. Imp? Did Eyja mean the horse? She had to, for no one else but her answered to that name. "In the field with the others, I imagine. Why?"

"No reason, I was just wondering," she answered airily. Then she bit her bottom lip as if a thought had occurred to her. "Who chose his name? Was it you?"

Trust her to always ask the last question he expected. It was one of her most endearing traits. He crossed his arms over his chest, amused. "Yes it was, as it happens."

"Why Imp and not Troll, Dáinn or Little Demon for example?"

"I don't know... The name just came to me."

Really she asked the most peculiar questions. How was he supposed to remember what had gone through his mind at the time? At least she seemed to have recovered from their awkward discussion the other day. He was more than glad to be discussing his father's horse's name rather than what they had done by the mighty oak. Perhaps against all odds she would actually do what he had asked and forget about the whole madness.

"Was it because of me? Because you call me Imp?"

He mulled over this a moment. He had truly never thought about it. "It might have been, I don't know. When Wolf gifted him the foal, that night *Faðir* asked us what name we would like to give him. Aife suggested Cabbage, but I think that was because we were eating cabbage soup at the time. She was only about ten then and she's never been very imaginative." He laughed. Unlike the woman in front of him, his sister had always been very sensible and logical. One had better ask her to look after a horse than name it. "After that, any name would have seemed better, so they all agreed to my proposition."

This didn't seem to please Eyja. It was as if she thought he was deliberately avoiding answering the question. He wasn't, he genuinely had no idea why he had offered the name, or why she had come today with no other purpose than to ask him about an insignificant event that had happened so long ago.

He had dreaded seeing her come to him with another lewd offer he would find impossible to resist and, though he was relieved to see that seduction was not on her mind, he found it hard to act natural with her. Asking her to revert to a more seeming behavior had been the sensible thing to do, but that didn't mean he found it as easy as she did. Getting things back to the way they'd been would require some adjustments. It struck him now that he had underestimated the enormity of the task.

"Why did you think of that word particularly, though?" She wasn't letting it go.

"Bloody hell, I told you twice, I don't know!"

But now that she'd forced him to think of it, Moon was wondering. *Why* had he thought of that name so easily? Was it because she was constantly on his mind? Was it simply because that day they had spent some time together? He snorted. Of course they had, it would have been hard to pick a day when they had not.

"Why do you want to know anyway?" She shook her head slowly and didn't answer. He didn't insist, only too glad to drop the subject because he really had no idea what to tell her. "How is your head?" he asked instead.

"Better, thank you, though I suppose I look a fright."

"The bruise is still impressive, if that's what you mean," he clarified. But that was not quite the same. She couldn't look a fright if she tried. "And at least the swelling is gone."

"Yes, it's not as painful as it was. And it's good to be outside in the fresh air."

As she spoke, she wrapped her cloak more tightly around her. It was bitterly cold today, but he knew she would not have let it deter her even if it had snowed. She had never been one for sitting indoors for days on end. She'd rather be roaming the land and hunting with a group of boys than sitting by the fire sewing or cooking.

"Aife told me you have a moon-shaped mark on your forehead now, one you might keep all your life," he told her with a smile. The idea intrigued him and he dearly wanted to see it but at the moment it was hidden by her hair. All he could see of her wound was the purple bruising reaching her eyebrow. "Is that true? Can I see?"

"No."

She took a step back, as if embarrassed by what she considered ugly. "Come, Eyja. I won't make fun of you if you do have a scar, not when it means that you were brave enough to save Gunnar and could have died because of it."

Keeping her eyes to the floor, she nodded her agreement.

Slowly, he moved a lock of golden hair to reveal the spot where the stone had struck her. And there it was, nestled in the middle of the bruise, an angry red crescent that looked remark-ably like his own. His sister had been right, Eyja would bear the moon-shaped scar all her life. It was just too deep to disappear without a trace. He didn't quite know what to make of the fact, except that it seemed significant somehow. Of all the shapes the scar could have been, it had to be a moon.

"What do you think?" she asked, still not meeting his eye.

"Yes, it is exactly like my own, only smaller. And I do think you'll have it for life."

Her shoulders slumped. "Is it very ugly?"

He couldn't help another smile. If ever he'd doubted she was a real woman, underneath all the bluster, there was the proof. "It's just as ugly as mine, I would say," he answered, knowing she would take exception to that.

"Oh. Not ugly at all then," she said in a breath.

"No." He brushed the little wound gently, then allowed his finger to trail along her cheek, her jaw, until it came to rest under her chin to hold her in place. "Not ugly at all. Nothing about you is ugly, Imp."

He bent his head, and then froze in shock, stopping just before his lips could touch hers. What the hell? Had he really been about to kiss her? Yes, he had. There was no pretending otherwise, or pretending she had been the one initiating it. It had been his idea, she had not done anything to provoke him. He had not even hesitated. One moment he had been stroking her scar and the next he'd lifted her chin up to him, bending his head as naturally as if they had kissed hundreds of times.

Why had he done that?

Once, he had feasted on her honey because she'd teased and goaded him into action, only the other day he had plundered her mouth because she'd offered to give him pleasure and would not take no for an answer. But today Eyja hadn't done anything. There had been no teasing, no goading, no scandalous offers.

She was just here, in front of him, looking lovelier than he had ever seen her, and he was the one doing everything.

He was offering compliments, *he* was stroking her, *he* was considering kissing her.

He was losing his mind, that was what he was doing.

Merely three days ago he'd told her he wanted them to stop acting as if they were lovers. She had actually heeded his command for once. And now, here he was, with his mouth a hair's breadth away from hers, about to devour her. His lips were even tingling in anticipation of this first kiss.

As slowly as he could, so as not to betray the fact that he had been about to kiss her, he inched away. It was probably too late for the move to pass as natural, Eyja would have understood what he'd been about to do, but he could not see any other way to act. He could not start apologizing, or explain an impulse he didn't understand, much less actually kiss her.

He had no other choice but to leave.

"Forgive me, I have to go. Elwyn is waiting for me at the hut. We agreed to..."

Having no idea what excuse to give her, he left mid-sentence.

Moon hurried through the village, feeling like a prized fool. His haste was such that he almost skidded on a patch of ice. He cursed under his breath as he righted himself. That was all he needed right now, to fall and break his leg. To add to his dismay, he then almost walked into Wolf, who was rounding the corner of the forge. They stopped before their bodies could actually touch, then each took a step back. The Icelander was looking at him strangely, and in that moment Moon had the awful impression the man knew he'd almost kissed his daughter—and was disapproving, which didn't surprise him. Relations between the two of them had been somewhat tense since they'd come back from war. Even after Eyja had revealed she was not with child, thereby proving that she was still a virgin, the tension had remained. Moon hated it, but he didn't see how he could change it.

After a brief nod, he veered toward his hut.

As if to punish him for the lie he'd told Eyja, Elwyn was actually waiting for him at the door, looking serious. Without knowing why, Moon knew he was about to ask about him and Eyja, something he had expected him to do ever since he'd walked in on them in the clearing. Considering how guilty and disheveled the two of them would have looked, his brother would have been a fool not to get suspicious. Accepting the inevitability of it, he invited him in. Nothing seemed to be going right today anyway, he might as well stop fighting it.

They sat at the table and he poured them both a cup of mead, pretending for as long as he could that this was only a friendly visit. Moon asked about Gunnar and his two sisters. Elwyn gave him all the answers he could have wished for. Then they fell silent while they emptied the remaining mead in their cups.

"So, what is it between you and Eyja? What were you really doing that day in the clearing?" Elwyn asked at last. The relief at having it all out in the open was palpable.

"I think you know, or you wouldn't be here, asking about it." Moon planted his gaze straight into his brother's. He might as well make the most of having an ally to try and see more clearly what was happening to him. It was time he stopped fighting this on his own. He needed help, he needed advice, he needed to understand why he could not seem to go back to how things had been with Eyja.

"I think I do."

With those words, Elwyn sat back in his chair. The message was clear. He would not help him along any further. Moon would have to bare his soul himself. No point in prevaricating. He sighed and went for it.

"Something has changed between us. It started while we walked to York with the army. I was forced to see her differently then and there has been no going back from there."

"You mean you started to take an interest in her because she was dressed as a boy? Mm, that is something to think about, little brother, don't you think?"

Moon did not appreciate the jest and threw him one of his coldest glares. "Do you want my fist rammed down your gullet now or do you want to hear the rest first?"

"Apologies. Please carry on. But for what it's worth, I'm not surprised you saw her differently when you were away from the village. It was the same for Bee and me. We'd gone to Mercia with Aunt Dunne and suddenly, all I could see was the woman she had become, and not the girl who'd always been by my side."

Always by his side. Yes, exactly.

"But how can we be together in that way? She's my best friend's little sister," he whispered. "Someone I have known all her life. I still remember the day she was born. El, I don't know how to deal with that."

Instead of answering Elwyn busied himself with pouring another cup, took a long draught, and nodded to himself. Then, just as Moon was about to explode with impatience, he asked. "Do you remember what you told me the day I told you I could not accept the feelings I was developing for Bee because she was my cousin?"

Did he remember? Moon blinked. How could he have forgotten? For weeks his eldest brother had been as gruff as a bear with a sore head, a very unusual thing for him, who was geniality personified. One day, unable to bear it any longer, Moon and Eirik had dragged him to one side to demand an explanation.

"What is the matter with you, then?" they asked bluntly.

The answer was just as blunt. "It's Bee. I think I'm in love with her." Elwyn crumpled against the wall of the hut like a man felled by a blow to the head. It was as if the confession he'd been holding in for so long had sapped him of all his strength. "I'm in love with my cousin, can you believe it?"

For a moment, no one said anything. Then Eirik spoke, his words slow and deliberate. "You know, us three are brothers, yet we all have a different father."

That was true. Although they had all been raised as brothers by Sigurd, Moon was his only true son. Elwyn had been adopted the day their parents had married and Eirik's father was a Norseman who had raped their mother a few weeks before that and had then been banished from the village by Wolf. A more unlikely family could not have been conceived. And yet the three of them were as close as if they had truly been born of the same parents.

"Yes, we were all sired by a different man, even if *Faðir* is our only father," he agreed, slapping Eirik on the shoulder in a show of support. His brother had always found it hard to know he was the product of their mother's ordeal, and no wonder. It was a heavy burden for anyone to bear.

But Moon understood what he was getting at.

"And in your case, you even have a different birth mother," he added, addressing himself to Elwyn. "Which means that, unlike us, you do not share any blood with Bee, if that was what you were worried about."

Apparently it was, because the look on his brother's face was as brilliant as the sun when the clouds parted after a storm.

"By the gods, you're right!"

Elwyn had turned on his heels, ran to Björn and Dunne's hut, and asked for their daughter's hand in marriage. The following day the two of them were wed, and less than eight months later, their first daughter was born.

"Well, you saved my life that day, for I was going mad with guilt and despair. I will now do you a favor and tell you the same thing you told me," Elwyn said, leaning in toward him like a man about to impart great wisdom. "You do not share blood with Eyja. She might be Torsten's sister, but there is nothing stopping you two from being together."

But it was not that simple. "You wanted to marry Bee, you were worried about your future children sharing the same blood and the problems it entails. It's not the same with me. I just..." He stopped. What *did* he want? He had no idea. That was the problem. He shouldn't even want anything.

"You just want to bed her, is that what it is?"

"No. Yes. I don't know. I mean, yes, of course, I want to bed her properly but it's not—"

"Properly?" Elwyn was quick to pick up on his unfortunate choice of words.

Moon merely stared at him, indicating he was not going to be any clearer. What had happened or not happened between him and Eyja was a private matter. Understanding he was not going to get any more information on that subject, his brother stood up and made for the door. Before leaving, he turned to face him one last time.

"Take time to think about what you want, but remember that nothing stands in your way if you want to be with her, in any way. Only you and your cowardice."

His cowardice. Moon blinked in incredulity. Had the man just said that? No one had ever dared call him a coward.

He was so stunned that he allowed his brother to walk out the door unchallenged. For a long moment, he stayed on his stool, staring into the bottom of his cup as if it could provide him with answers. It did not. In desperation, he poured himself another cupful of mead.

A moment later, there was a knock on the door. Elwyn, back for more insulting advice no doubt. Well, this time Moon would tell him where to shove them.

"You bloody idiot, I'll—"

He froze. Standing in the door frame was not Elwyn at all, but Wolf. With his fur cloak draped around his shoulders, the man seemed twice as big as usual. He would have appeared intimidating even without the scowl on his face. Moon's insides lurched. As if things were not bad enough between him and Wolf, he'd just called him a bloody idiot. Of course, the words had not been directed at him, but... It was hardly the ideal way to start a conversation.

"Halfdan. A word."

"Of course." Moon gestured at Wolf to come in. Refusing was not even an option. The Icelander walked in and, instead of sitting on one of the stools, remained standing in the middle of the hut. This would be a short visit then.

"So," he started. "Is there anything you want to tell me, other than I'm a bloody idiot? Or were those words not aimed at me?"

"They weren't," Moon confirmed, though it was hardly necessary. The Icelander would know this already and only wanted to unsettle him. But what did he mean? He was the one who had come to visit. Presumably *he* was the one who had something to say.

There was another pause, and then Wolf did speak.

"You seem to have gotten nervous in my presence of late. Or am I imagining things?"

No, he was not, but how could it be otherwise considering the way Moon's relationship with Eyja had evolved? It had been bad enough after he'd pleasured her but now... How could he not feel ill at ease in front of the father of the woman he had used so selfishly?

But it was not all this fault. Wolf had his share of responsibility in the new tension between them and Moon would not cower. It was one thing being nervous, quite another being, well... a coward as Elwyn had said.

He clenched his jaw, addressing his silent thanks to his brother.

"You're not imagining it, but you're probably not surprised, considering what happened after we came back from war." He paused, letting the words sink in. Wolf would have the honesty to remember and acknowledge he had almost forced him to marry his daughter and doubted his word that she could not be with child. It would be hard to recover from such an accusation. "And I cannot help but feel that you disapprove of me."

"Disapprove. Mm. Tell me, Halfdan. How would you feel if you were me?"

Moon cleared his throat but he had the fairness to admit that he would not take too well to a man who seemed to always be around whenever his daughter was in trouble. It certainly looked as if he was a bad influence on her. And Wolf only knew the half of it.

"I think I, too, would disapprove of me."

A nod. His honesty had been appreciated at least. Whether that would be enough to restore some trust between them remained to be seen.

"Now, on to the reason for my visit. Do you know a man from town called Cuthbert?"

The question was blunt, but that was not what made Moon's heartbeat increase in alarm. He'd asked Farmon's brother to send word when the Saxon was back. It seemed the time had finally come. His whole body tensed up, as if readying itself for battle.

"Yes. I do know him."

"He asked me to deliver a message to you. This is the message: 'Tell Halfdan that my brother is dead. His wife is safe'."

There was a silence during which Moon absorbed what he'd been told. Farmon was dead. Eyja was safe. They could both relax. This was the best news he'd heard all day. He didn't even ask if Wolf knew about the circumstances of the Saxon's death. It mattered not how and why the man had died, only that he would not come for Eyja now. His friends, Moon was not too worried about. Without their leader egging them on for revenge, they would probably forget all about the missed opportunity and focus their attention on other women to take their pleasure with, hopefully willing ones.

"What is that all about?" Wolf eventually asked. He'd obviously expected Moon to elaborate.

"It's... nothing to bother you with." Now that Farmon was dead, the Icelander would not be able to punish him for threatening and frightening his daughter, so there was little point in revealing what the man had done. It would only torture him unnecessarily. Moon would not burden her father with the knowledge of knowing how close Eyja had come to being raped by a pack of rabid dogs. He would be the only one plagued by nightmares over that notion.

"Mm. Now tell me, who is this wife of yours Cuthbert mentioned? Do not tell me it's my daughter." Wolf's eyes narrowed. "Have you been spreading lies about being married to Eyja, even though we agreed marriage between you was no longer necessary? Why?"

"No, it's not what you think."

"It's never what I think with you two, and yet apparently it's always *something*, is it not? Whenever trouble strikes, you two seem to be right in the middle, if not at the origin of it." He straightened himself to his full impressive height. "Well, no more, do you hear? There will be no more disappearing to war together, no more brawls in the middle of the village, no more coming back home bleeding and half conscious, no more lying about what you two mean to each other."

What was the man saying? Surely not what Moon thought?

Oh, but he was. Looking him straight in the eye, Wolf delivered the final blow

"I don't want you to see my daughter ever again."

"TORSTEN. CAN WE TALK?"

The two of them had not exchanged as much as a nod since he and Eyja had come back from war. A conversation was long overdue. Moon needed to feel he was regaining some control over his life. He'd been accused of cowardice by his own brother in the morning, he'd been forbidden to see Eyja in the afternoon, he wanted to do at least something right in the evening, to end the day on a more encouraging note. Making peace with his best friend only depended on him.

He'd seen him cleaning fish outside his hut and decided he was not going to avoid him any longer.

"Listen, I know you're angry at me for—"

"I was," Torsten cut in, looking just as tense and dejected as he felt. For the first time Moon realized that the estrangement bothered him just as much as it bothered him. It was a relief. He would have hated to lose his best friend over a misunderstanding. "I'm not angry anymore. I know that no one could have stopped Eyja from doing exactly what she wanted to do. And, in truth, I'm glad she wasn't on her own in the middle of all the men. I know you will have done all you could to protect her and I thank you for it. It can't have been easy."

Despite his wretchedness, a smile curled the corners of Moon's lips. Indeed the brazen imp was impossible to keep in line. That tongue of hers was enough to land her trouble at every turn. He should know.

"No, it wasn't easy, but there was no other choice. And I thank you. Your words mean a lot." It was a weight off his shoulders to know the air had finally been cleared. He'd hated the distance between him and his best friend. "I'm afraid your father is not so amenable though. He forbade me to see Eyja ever again."

There was a pause.

"She is his only daughter, and the youngest, that will be why. He is usually a fair and measured man but..." Torsten shook his head and sighed, as if loath to speak his mind because it felt disloyal to the man he loved and respected above all others. "Where she and my mother are concerned, he can be quite unreasonable, if that's the right word for it, because I'm not sure wanting to protect the women you love can ever be called unreasonable."

"No, of course," Moon agreed. He'd been desperate to see Eyja safe when they were only friends, so he could not imagine how he would have felt if she'd been his daughter or if he'd actually been in love with her. The thought made him frown because right now he could not for the life of him see how the urge could have been stronger. It had been visceral.

Torsten placed the last cleaned fish on the wooden platter and looked at him. "I'm sure *Faðir* will come around eventually, when he sees that being away from you doesn't make any difference to Eyja's behavior," he said, plunging his hands in the basin by his side. "She will be just as reckless as she's always been and he will see that it has nothing to do with you."

Moon wasn't so sure but what could he say? What was certain was that he would have to find a way to tell the Icelander he could not agree to such a decision. He had spent a week without seeing Eyja when they had come back from war and that had been bad enough. He wouldn't be able to handle more. To spend his life next to her without ever being able to see her laugh, hear her inane questions, or touch her soft skin, would be torture. To have to watch as she grew fonder of another man, perhaps ended up marrying him and bearing his children while he went from meaningless conquest to meaningless conquest would be hell.

If this came to pass then he might have to leave the village, as he would not be able to stand it. But... he didn't want to leave. This was his home.

Bloody hell, this conversation, which had started quite well, was starting to make him feel even worse than before. Perhaps it was time to put an end to it.

"It's freezing today," Torsten grumbled, rubbing his fingers over his braies to warm them up. "I can't remember it being so cold in fall. But, what do you know, frost burns as surely as fire. The only difference is you don't see it coming. It creeps up on you, and then before you know it, it's too late."

Moon was struck by the innocent comment. He'd always compared Eyja's eyes to frost and suddenly the comparison seemed hugely significant.

Like a revelation, an answer to all his problems.

It creeps up on you.

It certainly did creep up on you, slowly, inexorably, until it was too late. He was in love with the imp, *that* was why he wanted her safe, why the urge to protect her was so visceral, why he'd thought his heart had stopped beating when he'd seen her at the bottom of the dark pit and thought she was dead, why he could not bear the idea of never seeing her again or her being married to another man. They were not friends anymore, whatever he'd said, whatever he'd tried to convince himself. He would not have pleasured her so readily if they were, he would not have let her pleasure him so scandalously if he did not desire her like a woman, he would not have almost kissed her this morning if he didn't have feelings for her.

Everything within him surged.

Elwyn was right, nothing stood in his way, if he loved her and wanted to be with her. Nothing except his own cowardice.

Wolf had told him not to see her again. Well, Moon would do much more than see her, if she let him. He would touch her, he would kiss her, he would love her until there wasn't a breath left in her gorgeous body.

It was time to act like a man.

A month ago Eyja's father had ordered him to marry her, and he hadn't protested. This time he wouldn't do the same mistake. Wolf would be told in no uncertain terms that from now on, Eyja would be the only one allowed to dictate how much they saw of each other and on what terms.

After a nod in the direction of Torsten, he ran.

CHAPTER EIGHTEEN

Eyja raised her head at the noise of pounding feet and dropped the twig she had just picked up. Moon was running toward her in the fading light, as determined as any warrior on campaign, and it took her only one moment to understand what his target was.

Her.

Her heart sank into her chest. Why? What had she done now? All the things he had told her in the last few weeks came back to her.

You can be such a child sometimes. Stop plain annoying me. We should forget about what happened the last few weeks.

The biggest mistake I ever made.

And yet, earlier that morning, they had almost kissed. Say what he might, he had stroked her cheek and almost placed his lips onto hers. Even more importantly, he had initiated it, for once, not her. Was he about to blame her regardless, make it look as if she was somehow responsible for it, announce that from now on there would be no contact between them because she could not be trusted to respect his wishes to be nothing more than friends?

At this point she wouldn't put it past him.

He stopped in front of her, all bristling intent. By the gods, whatever ailed him, it was bad. But she knew in her heart of hearts that this time she had done nothing wrong. Except perhaps hope that he would change his mind about them being friends, but surely no one could blame her for that?

"What is it?" she asked, her breath coming out in swirls out of her mouth. It was freezing cold tonight but she could barely feel it, with her heart beating hard in her chest.

There was no answer. For a long moment, Moon just stared into her eyes. "Bloody frost", she thought she heard him say under his breath. Eyja braced herself for a mention of how her eyes were as hard as ice, or something equally scathing but he only smiled.

And then he kissed her.

Just like that. As if it was the most natural thing to do, as if they had already kissed a hundred times before and would kiss a thousand times again, as if it was all he wanted, as if he had never told her they could not be more to each other than friends, as if he knew she would welcome the kiss.

Which she did, with all her heart.

Her arms closed around his waist, her body angled toward his, her lips opened for him, her tongue darted out and started to dance with his. Everything about this kiss, which was not her first by a long shot, felt good, felt right. It was not too forceful, not too wet, not too bland. It was more passionate, more pleasurable, more significant than all the others she had shared combined. Her lips tingled, her blood sang in her veins, her whole body hummed. Moon tasted exquisite, like honey and spice, and felt wonderful against her, all hard and protective. If she'd suspected how good it would make her feel to kiss him, she would have sneaked into his hut at night long ago and forced him to give her what she wanted.

With a groan, Moon reached down to the back of her thighs and lifted her up into his arms.

"Hold on to me, I need more," he rasped, wrapping her legs around his waist to secure her in place and taking the kiss to another level, reducing her to a mass of need. Everything within her ignited. Could she ask him to lie down and—

A magpie squawked in the distance, shattering the moment into a thousand splinters.

"Wait." Remembering where they were, she tried to slide back to the ground, and found that she could not. His hold around her was too tight. No matter how much she pushed at his chest, he didn't budge an inch. "We should go somewhere else. If my father sees us like this, he will think we lied to him, and then he will force us to marry."

Moon spoke against her lips. "Let him try. He won't be able to force me to anything. No one can force someone to do something they have already decided to do."

"What are you talking about?"

Before answering, Moon took her mouth again. The sensation was too delicious for her not to surrender to his will. She allowed his tongue to spar with hers, her body to wrap around his like a vine After a long, lingering kiss, she managed to draw away. Before they did anything else, there was something she needed to know.

"Moon, *what* are you talking about?"

This time he allowed her some breathing space. "I went to see Wolf before I came to you. We had something to settle. You see, this afternoon he told me he didn't want me to see you ever again, as I was a bad influence on you."

Fury flared within Eyja. Her father had forbidden Moon to see her? And this after telling him he would never force her to do anything she didn't want to do? Well, forcing her to *not* do what she wanted to do was just as bad. Because she did want to see more of Moon. Much, much more.

"How dare he!"

In that moment she was glad Moon was holding her securely against his chest, because she was trembling so much she feared she would not be able to stand on her own two feet. Then a thought struck her.

A terrible thought.

"You didn't agree, did you?" she asked, her voice wavering, her heart fluttering.

Was that why he was here, why he was kissing her with such abandon, as if he didn't care about the consequences? Because it was a goodbye kiss and he knew there could never be others? Was he about to leave the village?

Moon deposited her back onto the ground and looked at her straight in the eye. "No, I didn't agree. In fact, I told him I could not live without you and asked if he would give his agreement to a union between us, one *we* decided this time. He said yes. I might add that he seemed rather happy about that development." He paused and twisted his lips in consideration. "I think he might have wanted to push me into seeing what had been staring at me in the face all this time. And... he called me Moon, something he hasn't done since we came back from battle, so I can safely assume he was not lying."

The silence following his words was as loud as the swarming of bees. Eyja was mightily... What was she feeling exactly? She hesitated between incensed, aggrieved and outraged, then realized it was more or less the same thing. She was furious, that was what she was. The wretched men, who both claimed to have her best interests at heart, had gone behind her back, talked about her future as if her opinion was neither necessary nor desired.

"You... You never thought to ask me first, before you went to see my father?" she exploded, incredulous. Didn't her opinion matter? This was her wedding they were talking about, her life!

"No." Moon tightened his hold around her, not in the least apologetic. "I didn't want to give you any chance of refusing me. You and I belong together, whether you want it or not, whether you agree or not. I will not stand by and wait for months for you to finally see it. You will be allowed time to come to terms with it if you need to, but that time will be spent by my side, in my arms."

In my bed.

The words were not spoken out loud, but she saw them in his eyes. She wavered and felt him steadying her. Even though everything within her melted, she refused to surrender so easily.

"Why would you even want me by your side? Only the other day you told me to forget what we had done." Did he have no idea of the pain he had caused her? "And I thought I was just an annoying imp? You've told me often enough."

He did purse his lips at that, even if he didn't quite appear chastised. "You are, but apparently, annoying imps are what I need in my life." He pushed aside a lock of her hair and stroked a finger over the bruise on her temple, lingering over the scar. "And I've finally found one, one that has been marked as mine. I rather like that."

"You haven't 'found' me. I was here all the time," she breathed, moved by the declaration. "I was always by your side."

"Yes. But I only truly saw you when you cut your hair and dressed like the warrior you are at heart. I love you, Imp. I might have loved you for a while without knowing it, possibly even all my life. Why else would I have agreed to have you follow us constantly, or have wanted to name our horse after you?"

"Oh, so I remind you of a horse, do I?"

"No." Moon's lips quivered. "Actually, you remind me of a goat. I was thinking of it only the other day. You, my love, are my own little, agile, stubborn, wild goat."

Joy bloomed into Eyja's chest. Why was she provoking him when he'd said all she'd wanted to hear, when she could see in his eyes that he meant every word of it? He'd seen her for who she was and still wanted her, still loved her. She reminded him of a stubborn goat and that was not enough to stop him. It could not be clearer, or more wonderful. He did not want her to be more feminine, less brazen, or easier to manage. He loved her just the way she was.

"I love you, too. Marry me."

A smile curved a corner of Moon's lips. "I'm supposed to ask that question, you know."

"It was not a question. It was an order. Marry me, Moon, now."

He shook his head slowly. "No. Not now. But in short order, I promise. For now, there's something I want you to do." He brought his mouth to her ear. "But let's go to my hut first. As much as I would like to do it here, 'tis too cold."

Her heart skipped a beat. Too cold. It was not too cold, as long as you were dressed, of course... So did he intend for them to be naked? The prospect made her heart leap.

"Yes."

Taking her by the hand, he led her back to the village. By the time they reached the door of his hut, they were both running. Eyja was breathless with anticipation. As soon as they were in, Moon kicked the door closed and took her back into his arms.

"Now. On to that thing I want you to do for me," he purred in her ear.

There was such wickedness in that statement that her breath hitched in her throat. If he wanted her to take him in her mouth again, she would fall to her knees in the blink of an eye. But the gleam in his eyes was more mischievous than carnal. So what? Would he ask her to open her legs for his kisses, the way he had in the forest? She would sit on the table and shamelessly lift her skirts if he did. Her whole body started to tingle at the thought.

"What is it?" she asked when she could not countenance the wait any longer.

"I want you to tickle me."

She stilled, torn between delight and disappointment. "Tickle you?" It was safe to say that this was not what she had expected him to say.

He nodded, suddenly serious. "That night near York, I stopped you from doing it and I was a bastard about it. But your body writhing against mine had pushed me over the edge and I could not deal with it." Ah, so he *had* been aroused. Eyja swallowed. "Now I would like you to do what you wanted to do and tickle me. I promise you'll like it, because you were right. I am rather ticklish, not that I would ever admit it to anyone other than you. And I won't tell you where my weak spot is, you'll have to discover that on your own."

Her throat had gone impossibly dry, but she managed to breathe. "I'm allowed to touch you anywhere I want?

"Anywhere." He allowed his gaze to wander over her slowly. "But I have to warn you. I will take my revenge when you're done.

He didn't need to say more. She fell on him, weaving under his arms and dodging his attempts at grabbing her, holding him by the waist, sliding her hands along his legs, his chest, trying to find a way to bring him down. Such was the intensity of the fight that they ended up rolling on the floor together. Half laughing, half groaning, Eyja did her best to expose that elusive ticklish spot. Moon howled when she discovered it was under the arms and triumph surged through her. Her victory was short-lived, however. Soon, he started to fight back in earnest and she understood that he'd been indulging her up till then, allowing her to explore his body and giving her a chance. No more. Now it was serious.

Breathless, she found herself pinned under him on the pallet, unable to move.

"This isn't fair. You said you wanted me to tickle you!"

"And you did, you lovely, maddening imp, you found out my weakness. But I warned you I would take my revenge..." Light flashed in his eyes and the hold around her wrists tightened. It was still not enough to hurt her, but it made it clear she was at his mercy. As if she would want to go anywhere... She was right where she wanted to be. "Now it's time I showed you what I have never done to virgins."

Everything within her dissolved. Finally, he was about to take her. And the best part was? She didn't even have to ask. They started to tear at each other's clothes in frantic abandon, only stopping when they were both naked and panting.

"Are you not cold?" Moon asked, glancing toward the firepit where only embers remained. "Shall I fetch more—"

"No." Thanks to their earlier exertions and the desire coursing through her veins, she was anything but cold. In fact she was burning. "Touch me."

"Ah, Eyja, you're just so... bloody perfect," he said, before cupping her breasts.

"You're not so bad yourself," she rasped back. Looming over her, all bunched up muscles and masculine intent, he was a sight to behold, a warrior about to claim his all too willing prize. She knew in that moment that she would never see him as just a friend ever again. He was her lover, and soon he would be her husband and the father of her children.

"You're mine, you know that?" he said, squeezing her breast.

"I do. And you belong to me, heart, soul, and body." That body was as hard as stone and the part jutting from between his legs unashamedly erect. She closed her fingers along the smooth shaft and gave a smile when he groaned his approval. "Nice snake you have here, by the way. I could just... eat it whole."

The laugh he gave was somewhat shaky. "All in good time, my brave girl. But you, too, have something I could just eat right up."

He gave one nipple a lick, then the other. Before he could lift his head back up, Eyja grabbed the back of his neck to keep him in place. This was too delicious, she was not ready to have him stop just yet. With a grunt he obeyed the silent but explicit instruction to suckle her harder. One hand slid along her stomach to come to rest in the place between her thighs. She was so wet his finger slid along the seam easily, parting the folds guarding her entrance. He started to circle it gently, before pushing in with slow deliberation.

"Yes!" She wanted that, she wanted more of him, and not just his finger.

Desperate to make him understand what she needed, she opened her legs wide and arched her back. But this time, instead of heeding her command, Moon stilled. There was an odd expression on his face.

"Would you rather wait until we are married to—"

"No!" she almost shouted. Why would she? They were destined to be together, and he was the only man she was going to lie with, so why wait another moment? "I'm dying for you." Or rather, she would die if he stopped now.

He placed a kiss on her throat, just above her collarbone then gave her nipples another slow lick. After his earlier suckling, they were hard as pebbles and almost painfully sensitive. "Are you nervous?"

No, not nervous, no. She let out a long exhale. Though she

was a virgin, she was not inexperienced, and she could not remember ever feeling this aroused. She would love anything Moon chose to do to her. "No. I'm dying for you."

"Do you want me to pleasure you first?" He started to kiss his way down to her intimate curls. The sensations he awoke along the way were exquisite but she stopped him before he could reach her navel.

"No, I'm dying for you."

"Would you prefer—"

"Moon, are you deaf? Haven't I been clear enough? I'm *dying* for you. Please, take me, now. I don't want to talk, I just want you to—ah!"

The possession was so sudden, so complete, that all the breath left her lungs. Well. She'd definitely gotten what she'd asked for.

Moon placed his forehead against hers in an apologetic gesture. "I'm sorry, my love, but you'll have to stop provoking me so, for I will always respond," he said, his voice raw with barely contained desire. "You saw when you offered me your mouth, I'm just too damn—"

She stopped him with a finger over his lips. "You're not 'too' anything, You're just the way I want you to be. And you did just what I needed you to do. Don't stop now."

"No."

He plunged inside her again, slowly. She bit her bottom lip at the perfect sensation. It was a tight fit, for certain, but she would not have called it painful, exactly. He withdrew and did it again, more purposefully. She rolled her head back in delight. They had only just started and she already knew this was going to kill her.

"More," she rasped.

Before the word was finished, he'd increased the speed, giving her what she wanted.

"Put your leg over my shoulder," he instructed, not slowing down. "I need to be deeper inside. You feel too good."

"Yes."

The change in position caused his shaft to rub in slightly different places, increasing her pleasure even further. Eyja bit her lip to stifle a scream. Moon stopped to kiss her, forcing her to soften her mouth again.

"No. Don't stop yourself, let me hear you this time. It's safe. We're safe, we're home. Please, sweetheart, moan for me, scream for me. Do what you need to do." He started to move again, giving her no choice. "Let me hear your pleasure."

She did. She could not have stopped herself anyway. Moans, each more lewd than the next flowed from her lips. When she screwed her eyes shut and threw her head back, floored by a wave of pleasure so intense she thought she would not survive it, she heard him rasp.

"Look at me when you come, my love. Me. I want to see you, and I want you to see me when I fill you up." Unable to resist such an entreaty, Eyja opened her eyes. Moon was looking at her with an expression she had never seen on his face. "For too long we have existed side by side without really seeing one another, but tonight I want us to see what we—"

He could not finish because right then her body seized around him, and his eyes caught on fire. All the air left her lungs and suddenly she couldn't scream anymore.

"Yes!" The groan he made when he stilled sounded as if it had been wrenched from his soul.

A heartbeat later, heat pooled inside her and she came again.

Moon had lost his body. There was no better way to explain how he was feeling. Numb, hollow and, above all, at peace.

Eyja was lying on the pallet next to him, looking barely conscious herself. His hand was wrapped possessively over her stomach. She smiled faintly when he started to rub it, as if she'd read his mind. This time she might well be with child. He'd certainly done all that was required for her to be. The notion made his heart beat faster. Now that he had finally understood and accepted what he felt for her, he could not wait to start his new life as her husband and father of her children.

Once his heartbeat had gone back to normal, he stood up, and went to get a cup of water and some linen to see to her comfort. When he reached his pallet and saw her stretched over the furs, all smooth, lithe limbs and alabaster skin, his breath got caught in his throat. She was so beautiful, so delicate. And he had possessed her like a demented beast.

"Don't you start," he heard her say.

"Start what?"

"In a moment you are going to apologize to me for the way you behaved. I can see it in your eyes. Well, I don't want to hear it. If I hadn't liked it I would simply have thrown you off me or taken a bite out of your ear." She lifted herself onto her elbows, daring him to contradict her. He did not, because she was right. She would have done those things and more if she had objected to the treatment he had subjected her to. This woman was a fierce warrior, not a meek maiden. "But I didn't want to throw you off. I wanted you inside me, deeper, harder, faster. You had better get used to it because it's not going to change anytime soon."

He could not help a smile. There was his impudent, brash imp. He had guessed she would make for a fiery lover and he'd been proven right in spectacular fashion. If she had been so wild on her first time, there was no telling what they would accomplish together in the future. Not that he was surprised. Hadn't Helga told him that she was tougher than she appeared? Yes, his little wife would be able to take him in all his impetuosity. Reassured, he started to wash her thighs with careful gestures.

"You didn't bleed," he observed, seeing no red on the cloth.

He felt her tense under his hand. "I swear I have never—" she started.

"No, I know you've never lain with a man." He believed her, without question. "Forgive me, I didn't mean it in that way, only that I'm relieved to know I did not cause you more pain than was necessary."

She relaxed and, closing her eyes, allowed him to wipe his seed from between her legs. "No, there was no pain, as such."

Mm, Moon mused, perhaps Thorfinn's caresses had breached her maidenhead a few weeks ago, or perhaps she had not had any to start with. A woman as reckless as she was, always riding or climbing trees might well have a different body than another, more sedate one. It didn't matter, in any case. It was better she had not experienced any tearing, since it meant she wouldn't have felt pain. At least no more than what being filled for the first time would have provoked.

"Are you not sore?" Remembering how he had thrust inside her, he felt a twinge of guilt. It had been hard, uncompromising. Say what she might, he would have to learn to control his most savage urges, at least until her body was used to his attentions.

"No, I'm not sore in that way, for your snake is not as big and strong as you seem to think." She laughed when he huffed in mock offence, knowing this was the reaction she'd been after. How wonderful it was to bed a woman with whom he could laugh. This was something new for him, and he already knew he would never be satisfied with less. Which was good because he was marrying his lifelong friend. "But I do feel as if I'd been trampled by an ox."

A chuckle escaped his lips. "Sorry, no ox, just me."

Her eyes opened a fraction. Not the least trace of frost remained in them, he was pleased to see. He'd melted it all for now. "How am I supposed to tell the difference? You weigh about the same."

"Imp!" That one word seemed to contain all the love he felt for her. He traced a line from the underside of her breast to her navel, then carried on over her hip before splaying his hand over the graze marking it. Apart from this reminder of her ordeal in the crevice, she was all soft perfection and he could not get enough of her. "You know, seeing your gorgeous body on display in front of me gives me an idea. One day, soon, I will cover you with moons and stars, just like you did when you were a child, and then I will lick them one by one, until you beg for mercy."

Eyja giggled, a delightful sound. "Then I'm afraid you will end up with a black tongue. Just like Hilda's ox. You really *are* like the animal, it would seem."

"I didn't say I would use coal to draw the shapes," he drawled, cupping her breast once more. It fit perfectly in his hand, proving they had really been made for one another. "I'm cleverer than a child, I should hope. I will use honey. And once my tongue is nice and sweet and sticky, I will—"

Too aroused to wait for the rest of the sentence, Eyja crushed her mouth against his in a fierce kiss. He loved how bold she was, how she felt under him, and on his lips. He loved... her.

"I will get some honey tomorrow, for our wedding night," she breathed, once she finally let go of him.

"Mm. A wonderful idea. But I think I'd better start practicing now, so I don't make a mess of things."

She stretched and opened her legs. "Yes. You had better do that."

In the morning Moon led Eyja back to the clearing where he had taught her to use the sling—and she had ended up introducing him to a pleasure he'd always dreamed of.

Heat invaded her body when he stopped in front of the tree with the moon carving. The place would forever remind her of their scandalous encounter. Not that she needed it. The moment was etched in her mind as surely as the moon was carved in the oak bark.

"Why have you brought me here?" she rasped.

Did he intend to ask her to drop to her knees? She would all too readily comply if he did. Last night Moon had not allowed her to renew the experience, no matter how much she insisted, instead lavishing his attention on her. She had been too lost in pleasure to complain but it would not be long before she demanded they recreate the moment.

He must have heard the breathlessness in her voice for he smiled and shook his head "We're not here for that, Imp."

"Oh."

"Don't be too disappointed. The day is not over yet."

Her whole body started to tingle at the promise. This time she would not let him distract her, no matter how skilled he was at it. She suspected he would not oppose much resistance, however, if she played her cards right. He had not last time.

"Before I do what I came here to do, there is something I should have told you yesterday. But between one thing and the other, I got distracted. Forgive me."

He took her hands in his and Eyja's heart started to beat faster when he looked at her. She knew that expression. Moon was fighting rising anger. That was the thing about getting involved with someone you'd known all your life. They simply could not hide anything from you, you always knew what they were feeling or thinking. And clearly, the news he was to impart made him angry.

"What is it?" Only a moment ago they had been laughing together. The shift in mood worried her. Moon must have seen it for he spoke, putting an end to the awful waiting in two short sentences.

"It's Farmon. His brother Cuthbert sent word that he's dead."

All the air left her lungs in one big exhale. "Dead."

"Yes. You don't have to fear seeing him anymore. You're safe, it's over," he growled. "He will never get to you now, and anyone else wanting to hurt you would have to go through me first, which will be no easy task. I will prove just as fierce as that giant on the bridge, the one no one but you was able to fell."

"Of this I have no doubt." She placed her forehead against his chest, relishing the sense of security he was offering. With this man on her side, she had nothing to fear. "Thank you. I love you."

"Don't thank me. It is my privilege and pleasure to be the one looking after you, loving you and pleasuring you."

"Yes." Three things he did better than anyone else. "And I promise to do the same for you."

A wicked smile answered her. "I do not doubt it. Now. On to the reason why we came here." He drew a dagger from his boot. "I'm going to carve a sun next to your moon because one is nothing without the other. I know that, because you are the sun to my moon, Eyja, the Sól to my Máni, and without you I am nothing."

Oh. The man had a wicked mouth that could bring her body untold pleasure, she knew that already, but apparently he also had a silver tongue... Surely it was too much for one woman?

"Sól and Máni are brother and sister," she said weakly, not quite sure how to deal with this new romantic side to Moon. The friend had been wonderful, the lover was something else entirely. "I don't think you see me as your sister after what we did last night, do you?"

He growled. "No, and I never did. Do you think I would have used your mouth the way I did if I saw you as a sister or even just a friend?"

Was he trying to kill her? "Stop talking about that, or I will want to do it again, and this before the end of the day."

He gave a throaty laugh that reached all the way to her core. "As far as threats go, this one is not exactly one to make me tremble. But first, I will carve a sun into that oak. From this day hence, it will be our tree and every time you bear me a child, we'll come back to it and add a star. I hope to be surrounded by our own constellation one day."

Eyja's chest tightened. This was such a beautiful thought that she could not help but fall in love with Moon all over again.

"Go on, then. I can't wait to see my sun beside your moon."

She watched him work slowly. One nick at a time, he made the shape appear in the bark and soon, a radiant sun shone in the crook of her moon.

He drew back to observe his handiwork. "What do you think?"

"Perfect."

The sun he'd carved was vibrant with life and energy, beautiful. Was that really how he saw her? Tears threatened to spill from her eyes. Ah, what was that man doing to her?

"*You* are perfect. So, let's go and get married, Imp," he purred into her ear. "And then, I'll fuck you until you can't stand."

The crude words sent her insides to the consistency of honey. She grabbed his tunic to draw him closer to her, and leaned her back against the moon and sun that would forever be linked, long after they were dead.

"No," she said in a rasp. If he thought he could tell her

something so shocking and leave it at that, he had another thing coming. She would never again deny herself—and him—the pleasure they craved.

"No?" He sounded just as breathless as she was and the part of him pressing against her stomach was impressively hard.

"First, you're going to fuck me right here, against our tree, until I can't stand. *Then*, and only then, will we go get married."

EPILOGUE

"**M**y first granddaughter." Despite the whisper, Wolf's voice was suspiciously hoarse. Eyja didn't move and carried on pretending to be asleep. Her father had been the first one to congratulate her on the birth of her daughter a week ago and she knew he'd been delighted with the new addition to the family. "About time, too. I've only had grandsons so far."

"You will enjoy having a little girl, you'll see," Sigurd, the other grandfather, replied, sounding just as awed. "And she's so pretty. Which is no surprise, of course, as she is the image of Frigyth."

Well, Eyja, for her part, thought that Emma looked just like her father, but after all, it could be argued that Moon was the image of his mother, so she kept her eyes firmly closed. Let the men think what pleased them. They clearly doted on the little girl, which was the important thing.

"You know what this means, my friend?" the Icelander asked. "You and I are now part of the same family."

She thought she heard the Dane clear his throat. Was he crying? Perhaps. She knew Moon's father had been orphaned at a young age and had craved a family while growing up. Now he had one, a large, happy one.

"That we are," he said. "I never dreamed I would ever have such a—"

"When you have finished mooning over Emma, you might want to come and help with the preparations outside." Her mother entered the hut and whispered to the men in mock disapproval. "Just look at you two! One would swear you have never seen a baby before."

Eyja fought hard against the smile wanting to bloom on her lips. Indeed, between them, the two men had welcomed their fair share of children and grandchildren throughout the years. You would have thought they'd welcome this one with more equanimity.

They vanished without a word of protest. Once the door was closed, her mother came to sit by the pallet.

"How long have you been awake listening to the two of them blabbering over Emma, then?" There was laughter in her voice. Eyja opened her eyes and frowned.

"How did you know I was awake?"

A smile. "You're my daughter, that's how. You will see how it is one day with little Emma." Ah, yes, probably, and Eyja couldn't wait. She held out her hand to her mother, who gave it a squeeze. "How do you feel? Will you be able to join us outside?"

"Yes, I should be fine."

"I will carry her if need be." Moon entered the hut, all masculine presence. Today his hair had been braided even more intricately than usual. With his neatly trimmed beard and his new leather tunic, he looked mouthwatering. "I will not have my wife missing the celebrations intended to thank her for the gift of my daughter."

Eyja smiled at him. The birth had been quite a scary and

difficult moment, because the little girl had been breached but Moon had been with her all the way, encouraging her, calling her his warrior wife, promising her she could do it.

"One day you will be able to tell our children what you did at Stamford Bridge, how you saved—"

"*Children!* This is the last child I'm having, do you hear me, Halfdan the Mighty?" she'd cried, as another, seemingly useless contraction had ripped through her. "You are not touching me ever again!"

And in that moment, she'd meant it. Until she had been handed the most beautiful baby she had ever seen, that was. Then she had grabbed her husband by the collar and ordered him to forget every word she had said in her delirium.

"Worry not, Imp, I already have," he'd purred, "except for one thing. How you called me 'Halfdan the Mighty'. I rather liked that, if you must know. And soon I will show you that I can live up to that name."

Soon. Unfortunately, she already knew it would take longer than she would like before that could happen. She had suffered quite bad tearing during the birth and lost a lot of blood. For days she had not been allowed to do much more than feed the babe and see to her personal needs. Helga, who had taken over her grandmother's role as village midwife as well as healer, had come to visit her this morning, to remove the stitches and had declared her over the worst.

Yes, thankfully, Eyja was starting to feel better and looking forward to her life as a mother in their new home. The move was planned for the following week, as Moon didn't want her to overtax herself.

In the end, with her husband's help, Eyja had built a hut with her own hands. Work had been slower than anticipated, however. The sight of a bare-chested Moon was just far too tempting, and she had found herself waylaying him more than once while they worked. Then in the last few months, heavy with child, she had been unable to do as much as she would have liked. Fortunately, her brothers had come to the rescue and the hut had been finished in time to house their babe.

When they moved in, they would leave Moon's old hut to Rorik and his new wife. His handsome cousin, who had seemed more suited to single than married life, had surprised everyone by proposing to the blacksmith's daughter a few weeks ago.

"Come, everyone is waiting," her mother smiled, picking Emma up from her cot. "Björn has just brought three casks of ale, Frigyth and Agnes have made piles of oatcakes, the children have woven garlands of flowers, Magnus has got the fire going, Dunne and Ingrid have embroidered banners to decorate the tables, and Caedmon... Well, I think he's made something special for the new mother but you'll have to see for yourself."

Eyja's throat went tight. "Please. It's too much. They shouldn't have gone to all that trouble for me."

Although she had attended dozens such celebrations over the years, she felt uncomfortable being the center of attention today.

"Nothing is too much for you, Imp." Moon lifted her in his arms and planted a kiss on her lips.

"Your husband is right. Besides, if it makes you feel better, it's not all about you. Rune and Eowyn have come to visit for the first time in years, to show the grandchildren their grandmother's country. We mean to make them proud. So come, let us celebrate."

Celebrate they did, all day under the pale winter sun and long into the night, surrounded by their families and friends.

After everyone had gone back to their huts, the new parents, their daughter cradled in a fur between them, watched as the moon shone over the sleeping village.

ABOUT THE AUTHOR

As far back as I remember, I have been attracted to the Middle Ages, to knights in shining armour and their ladies in spectacular dresses. Now I get to write about them, I feel like the luckiest woman in the world. Being French and married to a Brit makes each book I write extra special, as our countries share a long and sometimes painful past. But in the end, in life as well as in fiction, love conquers all!

I have published several medieval romances under my own name, including series, and also have a pen name, Judith Falcon, for spicier projects, still in historical romance.

Join my newsletter and check out my other books on virginiemarconato.com.

ALSO BY VIRGINIE MARCONATO

The Noble Norsemen

Taming the Wolf

Soothing the Beast

Wooing the Devil

Baiting the Bear

Tempting the Saxon

Seducing the Warrior